WAR PARTY

Fiction reprints published by Robert Bentley
in clothbound library editions

Nelson Algren
The Man with the Golden Arm

A. Anatoli
Babi Yar

Isaac Asimov
The Martian Way and Other Stories
Pebble in the Sky

Max Brand
The Stingaree
War Party

John Brunner
Stand on Zanzibar

Donn Byrne
Messer Marco Polo

Erskine Caldwell
Tobacco Road

Joseph Conrad
Almayer's Folly
Heart of Darkness
Lord Jim

Jack Conroy
The Disinherited

Marcia Davenport
East Side, West Side
My Brother's Keeper
The Valley of Decision

John Dos Passos
Manhattan Transfer

Theodore Dreiser
An American Tragedy
Sister Carrie

Erle Stanley Gardner
The Case of the Deadly Toy
The Case of the Gilded Lily
The Case of the Mythical Monkeys
The Case of the Singing Skirt

André Gide
Lafcadio's Adventures
The School for Wives
Strait is the Gate

Nicholai V. Gogol
The Overcoat and Other Tales of Good and Evil

Ivan Goncharov
Oblomov

Jaroslav Hasek
The Good Soldier Svejk

Evan Hunter
The Blackboard Jungle

Christopher Isherwood
The Berlin Stories

Charles Jackson
The Lost Weekend

Shirley Jackson
The Lottery

Ursula Le Guin
The Lathe of Heaven

Sinclair Lewis
Elmer Gantry

Jack London
John Barleycorn; or, Alcoholic Memoirs

Frank Norris
McTeague
The Octopus
The Pit

John Powers
The Last Catholic in America

Jean-Paul Sartre
Nausea

Budd Schulberg
Waterfront
What Makes Sammy Run?

André Schwarz-Bart
The Last of the Just

Clifford Simak
Way Station

Upton Sinclair
Boston
The Jungle
Oil!

Josephine Tey
Brat Farrar
The Franchise Affair
The Man in the Queue
Miss Pym Disposes

B. Traven
The Treasure of the Sierra Madre

H. G. Wells
The Invisible Man
The Island of Dr. Moreau
The Time Machine

Sloan Wilson
The Man in the Gray Flannel Suit

WAR PARTY

Max Brand

ROBERT BENTLEY
Cambridge, Massachusetts

Library of Congress Cataloging in Publication Data

Brand, Max, 1892–1944.
War party.
Reprint. Originally published: New York: Dodd, Mead,
1973, c1934. (Silver star westerns)
I. Title.   II. Series: Silver star western.
PS3511.A87W37   1981   813'.52   81–38502   AACR2
ISBN 0–8376–0460–5

WAR PARTY

CHAPTER 1

In weather like this, when the heat pressed like two thumbs against the temples, and the song of the locusts entered the brain with a dangerously rapid pulsation, Marshall Sabin insisted that his wife should wear a hat whenever she went out into the sun. But this day he was off hunting fresh meat, and she could overlook his wishes. She disliked the wavering of the soft straw brim up and down across her eyes.

He insisted that she wear moccasins, also, when she left the house; but her feet were as tough as an Indian's, and she decided that she would go as she was. Still, she was a little uneasy, for even when her husband was far away she felt the sternness of his eye upon her.

That was why, when she picked up the bucket and climbed the eight steps from the floor of the "dugout" house to the ground level, she paused at the top of them and ran her eye over the horizon with a thrill of childish fear and pleasure. Between the homestead and the edge of the world there was only the flat of the plain, with the shimmer and mist of heat-waves rising up from it. It was not often that she let her eye run out to the horizon in this way, because the immensity of it shrank their domain of ploughed land to a handful; so she turned her eye quickly to the cornfield, probing through the aisles and the dim shadows of it.

She was tall, but some of the lofty heads she could not

1

touch. Many of the big leaves were broken down, sun-yellowed, and they added a crisp note to the rustling, whenever the wind moved among the stalks. To her ear it was a sound richer than the noise of sweeping silks.

Her three-year-old son, christened Lawrence, but forever to be called Rusty by his father, because he had her own red hair, was out in the fenced pasture making friends with the calf, while the cow very wisely paid no heed to the child, but stood guard between her offspring and the big wolfish dog that sat at the bars. They had picked up the dog more than a year before, expressly as a playmate for Rusty, and they thought it amusing to name him Dusty.

She smiled as she thought of the coupled names, but the smile went out when she considered what labor it had been to haul the wood for that fence from far, far down the creek, and then to dig in the summer-hardened ground. However, if one is to have cornland, the animals must be fenced away from it.

She went on down the path which her feet, chiefly, had worn towards the creek. A puff of wind blew a strand of her red hair loose and across her eyes, so she slid the bail of the bucket up to her elbow in order that she might put that lock in place under the thong that she wore, Indian-wise, around her head. Above the knot of her hair the thong was joined at the ends by a green scarab pin that was her only bit of jewelry. Her uncle, that man of wisdom and wide travels, had sent the pin to her from Egypt. Her husband so loved the green stone against the color of her hair that she had formed the habit of wearing it constantly.

When she came to the bank of the creek, she looked down with a sigh at the shapeless flight of steps that had been cut into the ground, for it was a full thirty feet to the bottom, where the water was so thin a stream that it seemed barely sufficient to keep the pools full and fresh. The heat thrown back from the hard earth burned her skin so that she was glad, at last, to stand more than ankle deep in the water as she filled the bucket. There she remained for a moment, enjoying a breeze that somehow came wandering down between the sides of the ravine.

At the top she paused once more, but without putting down the pail. Even the touch of the hot wind was cool to her as it dried the sweat on her face.

She saw Rusty wandering towards the cornfield—forbidden ground—with the dog beside him. Moccasins and a pair of trousers were Rusty's outfit, and she smiled at the sleek, sun-blackened little body. She would have been happier if he had been heavier of bone and jaw and brow, like his father; yet she rejoiced because he was so wholly her child. His eyes were her eyes—deep blue—and one day the sun-faded brows would be dark like hers.

She went up the path towards the house. "Don't go into the corn, Rusty!" she called.

He turned to her gloomily, his right hand gripping the fur on the back of the dog's neck. Silently he watched her out of sight, and she was smiling as she entered the house; for she knew that in two minutes he would be twisting through the narrow corridors among the stalks. However, the dog always barked to give her warning, whenever Rusty went beyond the appointed bounds.

She had hardly put down the bucket of water when Dusty began to bark. And with the barking merged the scream of her son, wildly raised, continued, pulsing, though not broken by the beat of his running feet. Was it a snake? Was it that other danger of which Marshall Sabin had dared to speak to her only once?

On the table lay the revolver which he had freshly loaded before he left. She caught it up as she leaped through the doorway and up the steps. Confronting her was that second danger which, as Marshall Sabin had carefully explained, must be death for her.

Here, and there, and there, they broke out from the tall ranks of the corn. The sun burned hot on the red bronze of their bodies. The war-paint had turned their faces into goblin masks. Their yelling ran needle-wise through her brain.

Behind Rusty sprang a feathered enemy. She could see the anticipation in his grin as his left hand reached for the boy and his right hand raised his rifle as a club. Rusty, seeing her, screamed more loudly still, and threw out his arms.

She was perfectly calm; she was as steady of hand and mind as if these had been figures in a book, figures invented by the loose imagination of some writer. As she steadied the revolver with both hands, she heard a frantic outburst of yelling; but that was no matter. Rusty was right in the line of her fire, but that was no matter either. She had to strike her target, so she struck it. The feathered figure behind Rusty, as she pulled the trigger, leaped into the air with a hand clapped to his wounded face. Then he dropped to one knee and levelled his rifle.

Little Rusty, at the same instant, tumbled headlong. She got to him, somehow, scooped him up. To her, just then, he seemed to weigh nothing. She could have carried him in the grip of one hand, by the hair of the head; and with the other hand she could have fought her way.

She was at the head of the steps when the bullet struck her, but she would not fall. She got safely down into the house, before she collapsed in a corner. Dusty stood over her, trying to lick her face; and the boy was screaming again:

"Mommy, I'm hurt! Mommy, I'm hurt!—Look, Mommy! Mommy, I'm bleeding! *I'm* bleeding!"

4

On the sod of the steps outside she heard two muffled footfalls, like the steps of a heavy cart, so she stretched out the right arm, with the gun gripped hard, aiming at the door of buffalo hide. When it opened, she fired at the sun-flash on the naked copper of the Indian's body. He lurched on in, falling. He fell all the way across the room, dropping his rifle and striking his head and shoulders with frightful force against the opposite side wall. Then he slumped side-long on his face.

No more Indians tried to break through the open door, but she could hear the beat of their feet on the top of the house. The solid little mud building shuddered under the impacts.

She sat up, making three distinct efforts.

"Poor little Rusty!" she said, when she saw that the bullet which had driven through her own body had also scratched his shoulder.

The dog began to howl like a wolf.

"Mommy! Mommy! Look, look!" screamed Rusty, pointing, dancing with ecstatic terror.

She looked with dull eyes in the direction he indicated and saw the wounded Indian rising from the floor to one hand and one knee. She knew by the shaking of his muscles and the glare of his eye that the last of his life went into the effort of drawing back his knife to throw.

The mother in her saw that he was only a boy, smooth-bodied, supple. Looking down the sights of the revolver, she saw the poising of the knife, but she could not fire; she could only watch the pumping of the blood from his breast, and how it foamed on the floor.

Then the knife struck the floor with a shivering note of music, as though a gong had been struck at almost infinite distance. The Indian boy slumped to the earth. Yet he continued to reach for the knife, a tremor running through his

5

body, and he put his face against the ground and was still.

Dusty sat down beside the dead lad, pointed his nose rigidly at the unseen sky, and began to howl. It seemed to Kate Sabin that all the rest could be endured except the outcry of the dog.

She was in a stupor, from which a sense of unfulfilled duty pulled her back toward consciousness. She looked dully around her at the table which Marshall Sabin had made with so much care, at the broadbladed hoes which had flashed and chimed so many hours in the cornfield, at the little hanging shelf on which stood copies of the Bible, *Uncle Tom's Cabin*, and *Robinson Crusoe*. She had hardly opened the Bible except to record in the fly-leaf the day and the hour when she, unaided and with her own body and hands alone, had brought forth to life a man-child. This present pain of her dying, she realized, was far less than that agony had been.

There was a faint hope that this sun-blackened mite of a child would be spared, since the tribesmen sometimes adopted male children. If only she could dress him in his suit of clothes. Knowing that she had no strength for this, she pulled the thong from about her head and hung around his neck the green scarab. She prayed that in the eyes of the Indians the little green scarab might be a token of a great chief.

If only the howling of the dog could be hushed!

From outside, she heard the voice of a man, running towards the house and crying out in the Indian tongue some name or question, in a frantic note of grief. She could understand that, also; for there are not many sons in the tepee of a brave—and the dead boy was lying yonder.

She was seeing all this so dimly that she knew death was close. In her right hand was the revolver, with the muzzle pressed under her left breast.

6

"Rusty," she said, taking him in her arms, "they are coming—lots of Indians. But they won't hurt you if you're brave, and stand straight. Darling, kiss me—love me!"

He flung his arms around her neck and strained at her with all his might. If those had been the mighty hands of Marshall Sabin, it seemed to her that even now the outflow of her life might be stopped. But there was only the howling, the dreadful howling of the dog; the outcry of the Indian who was running swiftly towards the house; the voice of her son moaning at her ear:

"Mommy, Mommy, don't go away from me!"

What instinct told the boy that she was going away beyond call—forever? It seemed to her then that she wanted only one thing, and that was to see the face of the first Indian who entered the house, so that she could offer the boy to him with a gesture of supplication. But she dared not wait, because Marshall Sabin had told her that even though a woman was near death she was not safe from these Indians. So she pressed her face between Rusty's neck and shoulder, kissed his soft flesh and then pulled the trigger of the revolver as Marshall Sabin had taught her to pull it, with the squeeze of the entire hand.

CHAPTER 2

RUSTY SABIN, at eighteen, rode his horse behind Spotted Antelope up a ravine in the Black Hills. Although it was late summer, the water still ran strongly down the gorge, sometimes roaring like a wind, sometimes echoing from the walls like human voices. To Rusty Sabin, who knew himself only as Red Hawk, those voices rang with anger and reproaches, for there was wrath, he knew, in the heart of the Cheyenne who had adopted him. He had known it for years, and when he had asked Bitter Root, his foster-mother, what could be in the mind of the brave, she would answer:

"A wise man speaks only once, and not to a child."

However, he was about to pass from boyhood to manhood, since he must endure the torment and make the sacrifice of blood tomorrow. Therefore he knew that Spotted Antelope was about to speak at last; and in respectful fear he had been riding ten strides behind the Indian.

When they came to a place where the ravine made an elbow turn, Spotted Antelope dismounted and hobbled his horse, and Red Hawk immediately did the same. It was nearing sunset, but the mid-summer day was close and hot, so that when the gray old Indian gathered his buffalo robe close about him it was plainly no more than a gesture of ceremonial dignity. He pointed a shrouded arm towards a place where the current whirled in a deep pool, making itself smooth with speed.

"Purify yourself with water," said Spotted Antelope, "and afterwards I shall purify you with smoke. My son, you have made me unhappy, and now we are about to pray before the entrance to the Sacred Valley."

For some ordeal, Red Hawk had been nerving himself, but his breast grew hollow when he heard this name, for it was at the entrance to the Sacred Valley that Sweet Medicine, the hero who brought the buffalo to the Cheyennes, had last been seen by men. The foolish tribe had driven him out and had hunted him far away until, as he came to this gorge, before their eyes he had grown as tall as the clouds. His laughter had rolled from the sky, over the heads of his pursuers; and with one gesture of his hand

8

he had broken from the rocky wall a vast pillar and left it leaning, ready to fall on any who ventured near. Now, at last, the warriors understood what manner of man he was. And stretching out their hands, they called to him like children to a father.

The boy was full of awe of that legend as he pulled off his leggings, his moccasins, his breech-clout, until there remained on him only a green scarab which was fastened about his neck by a leather thong. Part of his name had come from it, from that talisman, for among the mysterious figures inscribed on the under side of the beetle there was a clearly drawn hawk. The other half of his name he took from his dark red hair, the long braids of which he now wound tightly around his head, and fastened.

He tried the cold of the water, and its force, with his foot. Physically, he was not true to the brawny Cheyenne type, who are the giants of the plains, though he was perfectly made for speed of hand and foot. Strength had been given him where it would best serve, and about ankle, knee and wrist the tendons were fitted close and neatly rounded off.

He looked at the obscure and shimmering bronze of his image as he leaned over the pool, his arms extended, his palms turned down, while he prayed:

"Underwater People, be good to me; and remember that I have sacrificed two good knives and an eagle feather to you."

Then he dived in, shooting himself out from the verge with a strong thrust of his legs. The currents were serpents that coiled on his body and caught at his hands, his knees, his feet. He went blind with effort before his hand touched a rock and he could draw himself shining and panting from the stream.

9

His father, in the meantime, had raised from a bit of tinder a small welter of flame. When Red Hawk had whipped most of the water from his body, he stood near the fire, into which Spotted Antelope was sprinkling sweet grass. Of the smoke he took imaginary handfuls and passed them slowly over his naked son, while the fragrance entered the nostrils of Red Hawk. It made him feel much better, and his heart grew lighter. He seemed to cast off evil and become a truer Cheyenne upon whom perhaps the eye of the mystical Sweet Medicine might fall with pleasure.

When this ceremony ended, Spotted Antelope led the way onwards, very slowly, for that is the way a man should walk when he wants the spirits to see his whole heart laid bare.

Thrice he paused, and at the fourth halt Red Hawk dropped without command to his knees, for they had passed the elbow turn of the ravine and he saw before him the entrance gate of the Sacred Valley. Red Hawk's mind conceived a form that extended to the sky and rested one hand on the leaning stone. He fell on his face, groaning.

After that, he dared not move. He had bruised his knees and elbows; the rock was cold against his belly; but he only ventured to unclose his eyes slowly, in order to see that his father—be his name praised!—had not left him alone in this dreadful place. Spotted Antelope now sat cross-legged, tamping the tobacco into his pipe with four ceremonial pressures of his thumb. With four gestures he stroked the stem of the pipe, fitted it to the bowl, and lighted the tobacco with a coal which he had brought from the fire of purification.

Therefore it was sacred smoke he drew at, his withered cheeks pulling into great hollows as he puffed.

Now he blew a breath to the ground, a breath to the sky, four breaths to the four corners of the world, and a

10

last cloud of smoke towards the gate of the Sacred Valley. The old man prayed:

"Listeners underground, be quiet long enough to hear me. Listeners above, take pity on me. Sweet Medicine, I am asking not for horses or buffaloes or scalps, but only honor for my son.

"If I have done bad things, I have already been punished. You know that Short Lance was my son, and that a woman killed him; but after she died I would not take her scalp because I saw a male child. He stood straight; he was not afraid; I took him home and gave him to my squaw. I knew that the spirits had taken away one son to punish me, but they had given me another because they did not wish to break my heart.

"I began to be glad. Red Hawk was both bold and happy. Soon he was the swiftest runner among the boys, and he could live in the water like a fish. The wild horses could not fling him from their backs.

"But I grew unhappy, for he left my tepee too often and sat beside the white man, Lazy Wolf, the interpreter and hunter, learning the tongue of the white man until he had two speeches—and is it not hard enough to make one tongue talk straight? Also, from Lazy Wolf he learned the same evil laziness of lying for hours looking at the fire as though it were herds of buffalo in a time of famine.

"In our proper ways, in practicing the scalp dance and in the sham battles he took no delight. For three seasons he has shrunk from the initiation and the sacrifice of blood without which he can never go on the war-path or be a man.

"Have pity on me, Sweet Medicine. I have tried to be a good man. I have taken scalps and sacrificed some of them. And now that I am old and my horse-herd shrinks and my hands weaken, let Red Hawk bring riches and triumph back to my tepee again."

11

With this the old man ended by pressing his hands to the ground, raising them to the sky, and extending them finally to the entrance gate of the Sacred Valley.

"Stand!" his father suddenly commanded Red Hawk, and the young man rose slowly to his feet. "Pray!" said Spotted Antelope.

Red Hawk wanted to pray that he should be given victory in war; many scalps; and above all, the counting of coups. But all he could find to say was:

"Sweet Medicine, give me whatever is in your heart to give to a Cheyenne!"

He had barely finished speaking, his hands were still outstretched when Spotted Antelope fell to the earth with a great cry. Red Hawk saw a miracle performed before his eyes. A great night owl sailed out past the leaning pillar!

The boy fell flat beside his foster-father, and close above him he heard the pinions in the air like the whisper of an unknown word.

Afterwards, with the cold of his dread still working in his spinal marrow like worms of ice, he heard the broken, gasping voice of his father muttering:

"Give thanks, my son! For this give thanks! Your prayer has been heard! Oh, son of my lodge, Sweet Medicine has heard your prayer and come forth to you."

CHAPTER 3

THE darkness was coming down when they returned to their horses, and the voices from the distant cataract in the Sacred Valley followed them down the lower cañon. Red

Hawk had not been allowed to dress. He had to keep his clothes in a bundle, all the way back through the hills until they came to the ring of plain in which the camp was pitched.

The moon was up, now, silvering the white new tepees. Through the entrances the rosy firelight made a step or two into the night.

Spotted Antelope, swathed to the ears in his robe, went on slowly, while the boy followed at a little distance. He knew that for his foster-father the world had been new-made; and in himself he seemed to feel the working of a new spirit, a transfiguring glory that could not be far away.

They went not to their own lodge, but to that of Running Elk, the great medicine man. Mysterious fumes of sweetness were rising from the fire in his tepee; the two squaws were at some beadwork in the firelight; and Running Elk rose on the farther side of the lodge to greet his guests. He was a tall, bent man; his long face placidly cruel and smiling with age. When he heard the story of the apparition of the owl, he made them sit down and smoke a ceremonial pipe with him, his low-lidded eyes constantly fixed on the boy. At last he spoke these words:

"It was truly Sweet Medicine. If he came out in kindness, then Red Hawk shall be so great that he can pull the rain down out of the sky and raise the buffalo from the ground for the Cheyennes. If he came in anger, then all the tribe will be shamed by Red Hawk and every father will give thanks that he has not such a son."

After that they walked to their own lodge, Red Hawk still naked. But no one looked at him, because it was clear, from the swathed form of the father and the bare skin of the son, that a ceremony was going forward or a vow being performed. Not till they had come into their own tepee; not till Spotted Antelope with trembling hands and a cloud of

13

smoke from sweet grass had purified his scalp shirt, his shield of painted bull's hide, Bitted Root, his squaw, his own person and the clothes of Red Hawk, did he permit his son to dress again.

The big face of the squaw, sodden, wrinkled, loosened by time, turned slowly from one of them to the other, as she sat cross-legged; she knew better than to ask a question. Red Hawk went to the great pot where buffalo meat simmered over the fire night and day, and would have helped himself, but his father forbade him.

Then, in phrases that were separated by moments of hard breathing, Spotted Antelope told his squaw what had happened, and what interpretation had been placed upon it by Running Elk. She, when she had heard, covered her face with a robe, as a decent woman should do when she hears of a mystery.

After a time, Spotted Antelope left the tepee. Bitter Root came to the seated boy and put her hands on his head, while her guttural voice prayed:

"Let the scalps of the Pawnees, O Underground Listeners, O Listeners Above—let the scalps of Pawnees hang from the center pole and dry above our fire!"

She had not turned her thoughts to glory or riches, for Bitter Root was a practical woman.

When she in turn was gone, Red Hawk leaned against a feathered backrest for a time, gloomily. His stomach raged for the food that had been forbidden. He thought of unrolling his bed and lying down to sleep. Instead, he suddenly found himself on the way to the tepee of Lazy Wolf.

At this season of the year, Lazy Wolf's tepee was different from the others. In the winter the white man might use a regular lodge of the skins of buffalo cows, but in the summer he used a strong, light canvas.

The firelight glimmered through its frailer texture as

Red Hawk stopped outside the entrance flap. The cheerful voice of Lazy Wolf called him in at once.

As usual, he reclined on a heap of buffalo robes, with a book resting on his stomach. A lantern gave him light. It was fed with a strange, treble-refined fat which was odorless, and the flame was protected by a stretched, transparent membrane. Red Hawk had seen the contrivance many times before, but it remained a great marvel, and a strong evidence of medicine.

Blue Bird, the daughter of the white man, merely turned and smiled at the visitor. She had hair and eyes as dark as those of her Cheyenne mother; but the hair was like wavering silk, and she had that olive complexion which is easily illumined. To Red Hawk, she was the chief miracle to be found in the tepee of Lazy Wolf; and because he feared her, he always joked a good deal when she was near.

She was stirring the meat pot over the central fire. It was not such a huge affair as that which appeared in the lodges of the Cheyennes, and in this summer weather merely a handful of flames was maintained beneath it; but out of that small cauldron there came savors more varied and pleasant than the greasy eternal smell of stewing back-fat and dried buffalo meat.

Now, unless the sensitive nostrils of Red Hawk betrayed him, the flesh of small birds was seasoning and softening in that pot. He turned, half faint with hunger.

"Sit down by me," said Lazy Wolf, turning on one elbow, but not enough to disturb the comfort of his fat paunch, on which he laid his open book, face down. "Sit down here and tell me the news of your ride."

He pushed a pair of spectacles up on his forehead and looked at Red Hawk with his misty blue eyes. He began to comb his beard. He never shaved himself clean; he merely shaped, from time to time, the hair that grew on his face.

15

All day long his fat fingers would be curling and uncurling it. Truly, he had earned his name of "Lazy," for he never bestirred himself except to hunt a little, now and then. He rarely went to the feasts; he took small part in the ceremonies; and above all, he would never go on the warpath.

He was valued by the Cheyennes, however, for three important reasons. One was that he was a perfect interpreter and a shrewd trader in their behalf. Another was that in time of winter famines his accuracy at long range made his rifle worth more in getting meat than all the guns and arrows of the tribe. Finally, when on two occasions the Pawnees had found the camp stripped of its young warriors and had tried to rush it, the guns of the white man had seemed to be everywhere. That was why they dealt out to him his full name of "Lazy Wolf." He was prized, revered, and at the same time despised by all the Cheyennes.

Red Hawk sat down against a back-rest and lounged. He pulled out a long, heavy knife and began to spin it in the air, so that it came down on its point, almost always with the first try. No man among the Cheyennes could rival him in that clever trick. He did it with the air of indifference; but when his eyes rose following the flash and spin of the blade, they always flicked aside a trifle in the hope of finding admiration or wonder in the eyes of the girl.

However, as usual, she was a disappointment; she seemed to regard his knife-work as no more than so many conventional gestures of the hand.

"There is not a great deal for me to tell, Lazy Wolf," said Red Hawk. "What has happened in the camp?"

"There is not a great deal for me to tell, either," said Lazy Wolf, smiling a little. "But the three braves who went towards the western mountains still have not come back, and people are saying that Wind Walker may have met them."

"Could Wind Walker kill three Cheyenne braves?" asked the boy, staring.

"He's done it before," answered Lazy Wolf. "He has twenty-five scalps to his credit, people say."

"You, Lazy Wolf, are a white man," said Red Hawk, angrily.

"So are you," smiled the other.

"But my heart is all red!" exclaimed the boy.

"Good!" cried the Blue Bird, and he thought that the fire could not light her eyes as much as they shone now with her smiling.

"Besides," said Lazy Wolf, "I have seen the scalps and have talked to Wind Walker."

"Without aiming your rifle at his heart?" cried Red Hawk.

"You have to understand what I've told you before," said Lazy Wolf. "I am only a Cheyenne while I'm in their camp. But if it makes you any happier, I'll tell you that Wind Walker hates me because I stay with the tribe, and therefore I can't like him very well. As a matter of fact, I went to see him in the hope that I could find out why he spends his life hunting down the tribe."

"And why?" demanded the boy.

"Because he happened to have a wife who was murdered by the Cheyennes—there's the only reason. Some white men put a value on women. Not I—but some white men like their wives and daughters better than herds of horses and hundreds of scalps." He laughed and looked at the girl. "Give Red Hawk some food," said Lazy Wolf to her.

"My father says that I should fast," answered the boy.

"In your father's lodge, therefore, you ought not to eat. But this is a different tepee, and I can see by the way your nostrils tremble when the steam of the pot blows to them that you're starving. Blue Bird, give him some of that stew."

17

Her lips and her eyes parted for a moment before she could cry out, "No! Spotted Antelope has given commands."

"In his own lodge. But this lodge is mine," said Lazy Wolf. "Bring him some food!"

She brought two bowls, one filled with a stiff mash of cold boiled corn and the other with the stew; then she retreated, walking backwards, her eyes fixed on Red Hawk so that he actually seemed to feel them, like the touch of a hand. Suppose he should so much as look at the food, how would he sink in her esteem to the level of a disobedient son!

So he turned his head towards Lazy Wolf, saying, "What is the white name of Wind Walker?"

"Marshall Sabin," said the other. "He is a big man, my lad. Not young now; a good forty-five years old. I should say. But he is as tough as ash and oak. By his hands and his jaw and his eyes you can see that he's a man-killer.

"Some of your warrior Cheyennes are bigger men, and younger; but I wouldn't gamble on their chances if he managed to get a grip on them. Are you wasting that good food, you hungry coyote?"

Lazy Wolf smiled. He was always smiling, making light of the most sacred of the Cheyenne customs, which was the reason that old Running Elk hated him.

"I think of my father," said the boy uneasily.

"Then I shall take the food away," broke in the girl, hurrying across the lodge.

"No, let it alone," commanded Lazy Wolf. "Perhaps he'll change his mind. And now that he's about to become a man, it's good for him to endure temptation."

The father began to badger her, saying, "If she obeys her husband as well as she wants you to obey your father, she'll make a fine squaw for one of the bucks. And she's fifteen,

Red Hawk. High time that she should marry and let me make a little profit on her. There was Crazy Bull, only this morning, who tied eight horses outside my lodge.

"But I had to let him take them away again. And yet there were eight of those horses against the girl—and they were good ponies, too, the pick of his herd. Crazy Bull spread out enough bright beads to cover three suits of clothes. But I had to let those go, too, because when I looked at Blue Bird, she was making faces."

"Crazy Bull is a very strong brave," said Red Hawk. "True, he has a broken nose; but he is a great hunter. He has a good many children in his lodge, but he has three old squaws to take care of them. You should marry Crazy Bull, Blue Bird."

"I would," answered the girl, "but I can't leave my father with no woman to take care of him."

"Tut, tut!" said Lazy Wolf. "I would have a good handy squaw in the lodge in no time—a thorough worker, and one with hands that are busy all day long.

"There's Grass Woman, for instance, who has gone back to her father since Wind Walker met her husband, one bright day. For one horse—for a colt, even—I think I could buy her. And she's the proper type; built close to the ground, and able to bear burdens. She would never waste her time making dresses of white doeskin that fit her body to the hips as though she had dipped herself in water—and all for the sake of honoring the initiation day of a boy—a mere long-legged, time-wasting boy named Red Hawk."

Red Hawk sat up and looked at the girl; at the white doeskin dress that held the roundness of her body as the skin holds a fruit, and then flared out in a wide skirt of many folds. It was true, he suddenly realized, that she was fifteen and marriageable, according to the Cheyenne custom. She was looking at her father with a quiet eye, dark-

19

ened by anger, but the flush began to run up her throat and over her face.

"Lazy Wolf will still be talking," said she, "but talking won't raise the sun."

"Look Red Hawk in the eye, if you dare," said Lazy Wolf. "Look him in the eye if you can, and tell him that the dress was not made in honor of his day!"

She turned her head towards the boy; but before their eyes met, she gave up with a faint cry and ran out of the lodge.

Red Hawk sprang to his feet, remembered himself, and sat down trembling.

Lazy Wolf continued to stare, rather gloomily, towards the entrance flap, but he said, "Now eat, my son—and tell me what is in your mind."

Red Hawk hesitated. He wanted very much to follow the wishes of his father, but the advice of Lazy Wolf swayed him like a wind; and just now a special fragrance rose to him from the delicious stew. Instantly his grasp was on the bowl.

CHAPTER 4

WHEN he had eaten, there was some shame in his mind, but much contentment in his belly. He washed his hands; filled a pipe, without ceremony, and smoked it in long, slow puffs. He told his friend the story of the day. When he had finished with the prophecy of Running Elk, such an awe came over him that he shuddered, unable to lift his eyes from the ground. Then he heard the careless voice of Lazy Wolf saying:

"The twilight, of course, is the proper time for an owl to go out hunting; and you were in front of the valley gates just at sunset. That owl was not the spirit of Sweet Medicine. He was just a big hungry stomach that was thinking neither of Red Hawk nor of Spotted Antelope, but of field mice and rabbits or anything else he could get into his maw."

The heart of Red Hawk fell.

"I was brave because the owl flew over me, but now I'm afraid again," he said. "Yet there was a spirit in the bird. His wings stretched farther than across the floor of this lodge. His eyes were golden balls of fire. His wings whispered as he slid over my head and said a word."

"Well," said Lazy Wolf, "if the flying of that owl gives you any comfort for tomorrow, keep on believing in it. Are you afraid of the blood sacrifice, my lad?"

Red Hawk half closed his eyes. He realized that the answer was a thing which he could never endure to speak to any Cheyenne; but it was easy to confess even shameful truths to this man. Therefore he gasped:

"I am afraid! I think I could stand the cutting of my flesh, even with the notched knives, and the tying of the ropes into my body. But when I think of how they must be torn out again, I am sick!"

"I would be, too," said this surprising hero.

"You? Even you?" exclaimed Red Hawk. "But you are a white man! Only your name is Indian."

"At least," said Lazy Wolf, "there are a few brave men among the whites—like Wind Walker. He is brave exactly as the Cheyennes are. You remember when he was captured once and tortured, they could not make him stop cursing them and daring them. Yet before the soldiers broke through the camp and saved him, he had been hanging on the pole for two hours. He is brave like the Indians.

21

"But there are no white men who have ever gone through the blood sacrifice which you're going to make in order to prove that you're able to be a man and a warrior. Every white man in the world would have disgust up his nostrils and in his bowels at the mere thought of giving his body to be tormented."

The flames of the fire leaped for the last time. Red Hawk, puzzled, merely said:

"For the white face and the white mind there is one world; but when the *heart* is red, there is another."

He stood up, for suddenly he wanted to be away from this lodge before he had to endure again the quizzical smile of Lazy Wolf.

"Go on, my lad," said the other. "If I thought that it would do you any good, I'd go to the lodge tomorrow and look on through all that beastliness for the sake of cheering you along. But after the first knife cut, nothing will be of any use to you except a crazy, red-eyed frenzy. Good-night. Sleep if you can; and if you have to go through with the torment, try hard to make a wild man of yourself."

Red Hawk went out into the night. As he stood outside the entrance flap, looking over the moon-washed hides of the tepees, and at the stars which scattered down towards the dark horizon like golden sparks, he thought of Blue Bird; and it seemed to him that her touch and the sound of her voice alone could cure his lonely fear.

However, it was a matter about which he must see men. Only the day before it had appeared to him that he had a hundred friends. But in this time of need the many shrank to two. Of these, Lazy Wolf had merely smiled and bantered. There remained the second friend, Standing Bull.

Already, at twenty, Standing Bull was a famous warrior because of an exploit of the year before, when, in the narrows of a ravine at sunset time, as he fled with a companion before the rush of a war-party of Pawnees, his friend had been wounded and the youth had turned back to hold the narrows until the injured man could draw away. With his rifle and lance he had killed two of the Pawnees, had counted grand coup on both, and had secured the scalp of one of them. For that heroic effort he was given the name of Standing Bull.

In front of the lodge of his friend, Red Hawk now paused. Within, the brave was chanting a song, very softly:

> "Braid your singing with my song
> And the music will be strong."

And the voice of Bending Willow, the wife of Standing Bull, joined with an undertone in the chorus:

> "One voice cannot rise so high,
> But two voices reach the sky."

Then Red Hawk, unwilling to hear more by stealth, called, "Standing Bull, a friend is at your door."

Bending Willow cried out in alarm, but Standing Bull said:

"It is only Red Hawk. Hush and be still. Come in, my friend."

Red Hawk entered, instantly drawing shut the entrance flap behind him, for he saw the girl reclining on a willow bed, still half struggling to raise her head from her husband's lap, while he restrained her and continued to brush her hair with a porcupine comb. As a last resource, she tried to throw the corner of a robe over her head, but Standing Bull prevented this, also, saying:

"This is my friend, Red Hawk. Lie still. Hush! He wants no greeting. Sing some more of the song. If Red Hawk is

23

to be a brave tomorrow, he will want a squaw the next day, and he will need to know love songs!"

In a moment the three were laughing and singing, while Red Hawk capered around the fire in a slow dance which he finished by kneeling in front of his friend, and crossing his arms on his breast.

The brave now stood up, and Red Hawk extended one hand to him. Looking up, he saw nothing but the ragged scars on the breast of Standing Bull, the proof of how he had torn the rawhide thongs out of his flesh quickly at the blood sacrifice. He had made it in his fourteenth year. He was big, with a shoulder like a buffalo bull, and legs like a deer's, for speed.

"What is it?" asked the warrior. "If you hold out your hand to me, take whatever I have to fill it. There are nine good horses tethered outside my lodge; they are yours. There are two rifles—and knives—and that bag is filled with beads. You see the pemmican, the dried meat, the knives, the robes, the back-rests. Whatever I have is yours, except the scalp of the center pole, and the coup stick and the shield and the medicine bag. These are my medicine, and they would not be good for you. But if you want something more, tell me and I shall kneel with you and pray for it, or go out with you to fight for it."

Red Hawk looked higher still, into the face of his friend. There was still a boyish softness and beauty about the features of Standing Bull. It was only when he stared fixedly, as now, that one could see how the eyes grew dangerously bright.

"I have not come to beg for horses or guns," said Red Hawk. "I want some of the strength of your heart."

"You would have it all, if I could dip it out with both hands and pour it upon you," answered the brave. "I still remember, whenever I see still water, how the Underwater

24

People fixed my feet in the quicksands, long ago—six years, or five years ago. All the other boys were gone from the side of the pool except you, and you were small. Nevertheless you dived for me, like a bright fish. You tangled your hands in my hair and jerked me free. We swam to the bank and lay gasping and biting at the air. With every breath I tasted, I knew that life was good, and that you were my brother. When you are a warrior, Red Hawk, we shall exchange blood, and after that we shall be like the son of one mother."

At this, Red Hawk looked suddenly down because tears were stinging his eyes.

He was able to say, at last: "Tomorrow I must go into the Medicine Lodge to make the sacrifice. I am weak at heart, Standing Bull."

He heard Standing Bull sigh. The sinewy hands of the Cheyenne raised him to his feet. "Come," said the warrior. "We shall go out and face the east until the sunrise, and I shall give you strength."

But as Red Hawk left the lodge, he saw the eyes of the young wife lift from the beading of a moccasin with a flash of scorn. That glance kept rankling coldly in his vitals, all the way to the low hillock outside the camp, where he stood with Standing Bull through that night, facing east.

When the color of the dawn began, the warrior took his hand and held it, as the huge brilliance rolled over the edge of the earth and started up the hill to heaven.

Red Hawk smiled as he looked at the display. His hand was warm from the clasp of his friend; and he felt that borrowed strength had filled his heart.

CHAPTER 5

WHEN Red Hawk returned to the tepee of his father, he found the sixty-year-old warrior doing a hatchet dance around and around in narrow circles before the lodge, now and then springing into the air to strike down enemies. Other people passed back and forth before the tepee, never regarding the dancer. The younger boys were taking out the horses of the camp to graze, but they would be back in time to enjoy the spectacle of the blood sacrifices.

Spotted Antelope stopped dancing when he saw his foster-son. "You are almost late!" he called to Red Hawk. "The sacrifices already have begun, and you must be painted. Quickly, my son!"

They hurried to the lodge. Outside were women and children, waiting for the happy moment when some tortured youth fainted in the lodge and was taken from the enclosure to be dragged around and around at the end of a rawhide rope tied into his flesh. Then the young boys would throw themselves at the prostrate body so as to jerk it free; and if that failed, the horseman halted, backed up twenty feet, and made his pony bolt away at full speed. The whiplash at the end could not fail to tear the rawhide free from the tough flesh. More than once, from his childhood on, Red Hawk had seen that ceremony, and the dull noise of the rending flesh was still fresh in his mind and felt in his body.

Now he was entering the medicine lodge, making the proper ceremonial gestures, aware of the customary trappings of the rite. He looked at the gaudy center-pole; at the two naked Indian lads who already were tied to it by long thongs. Dancing, chanting loud prayers, from time to time they wrenched back their weight in an effort to tear out of their flesh the ropes that had been tied into their pectoral muscles. For the more quickly a man freed himself, the greater his honor, the more perfect his prayer.

Not far away, Running Elk was now at work with two more candidates; and the blood which ran down the scrawny arms of the medicine man dripped steadily from his elbows. One glance showed thus much of the picture to Red Hawk. After that, with black mist spinning before his eyes, and with sagging knees, he looked down at the paint which Spotted Antelope was putting on him. There was a band of red, half an inch wide, painted around the body just above the hips, and another around his right arm just below the elbow. On his breast appeared a sun, with red rays running from it to the hips and shoulders. His forearms and legs were now being reddened, then the trunk would be blackened except where the other designs had been drawn.

The heart of Red Hawk was soothed by these lavish adornings; this magic made it impossible for him to fail in the ordeal. Red Hawk knew of but one Cheyenne who had blenched under the torture. That unfortunate was literally a nameless creature, never to be mentioned, never to be called by the crier to a feast or a ceremony, never taken on the warpath, never admitted to the medicine lodge.

The painting had ended.

The tall form of Standing Bull came to his friend and took his hand.

"Look on your own blood," said Standing Bull, "as though you looked upon the blood of your enemy. Do you think that the spirits can fail to see? As the blood runs from you, the beat of your feet will be on their breasts, and their ears will be opened as you pray to them for glory for scalps, and for many coups."

He stepped closer and murmured, "Breathe deeply; look high. Think of your spirit as of the mountains, and of your flesh as the grass that dies on them every year. I shall pray for you, brother."

It seemed to Red Hawk that he was smiling in answer, and murmuring thanks; then he found that his father had led him close to Running Elk and had retired. He was alone. His knees shuddered. Was it the smoke that made him choke?

He saw, in front of Running Elk, a lad of fourteen whose boy-name was Leaping Frog. He was a half-deformed, stunted youngster with very wide shoulders and a meager, starved body. The bony roundness of his face had given him the important half of his name. Now, as Running Elk laid hold of the right breast of the boy with thumb and finger, pulling out the loose skin, the Frog caught the glance of Red Hawk and pointed into his own eyes, smiling an invitation to watch closely and see if even the flicker of a lid gave token of the pain he was about to endure.

Running Elk slashed quickly on the right and on the left of the flesh which he held. Blood spurted, but as Red Hawk stared into the eyes of Leaping Frog, they smiled calmly back at him while the medicine man drove the knife through between the cuts. With two fingers the old man stretched out the band of loosened flesh, carelessly, like one handling dead meat, so that he could easily pass under the loop the end of a strong rawhide thong which he now tied, drawing the knot up hard. Still Leaping Frog continued to smile.

A hand grasped Red Hawk's own right breast. He looked down and saw the bloodstained hand of Running Elk. Even the eyes of the terrible old man seemed to be washed in blood.

"Wait!" said Red Hawk, gasping. "There is someone else to come before me. There is Leaping Frog to finish."

"Ah—dog!" said Running Elk. "It is true that Sweet Medicine flew over you; but it was his shadow that he trailed over your spirit. Hear me, son of Spotted Antelope!"

He raised his voice suddenly, so that it ran through the whole of the Medicine Lodge and brought upon Red Hawk a dreadful battery of eyes. The drumming ceased, or fell to a murmur that was fainter than Red Hawk's thundering heart. Even the dancers around the center-pole of the lodge stood still, frozen with dread lest a frightful disgrace now fall upon the tribe.

"Do you give yourself freely?" shouted Running Elk. "Do you give your body freely to the knife?"

The words began to ring back and forth through the mind of Red Hawk like windy echoes that fly down the narrowness of a ravine. He parted his lips, and thought that he had said "Yes!" But the blood-dripping hand of Running Elk was still held high in suspense.

Then a faint voice drifting across the air touched Red Hawk's ears, for it was saying: "Strength! Give him strength! I offer six good horses—I sacrifice a beaded shirt and a new rifle—"

That was Spotted Antelope, praying for more than the worth of his soul.

"Answer!" thundered Running Elk.

Red Hawk's head dropped; his knees sank under him and the knife of Running Elk cut the air just before his face.

"Go out of the lodge!" cried the infuriated medicine man. "It is forever closed to you. I see the face of a man and the heart of a dog. Sweet Medicine has breathed darkness over you; your name is forgotten in my ears!"

The drums suddenly began to beat; the dancers moved again around the center-pole, shouting their prayers; but what Red Hawk heard as he turned towards the entrance was a cry of grief, short and sharp, wrung from the heart of an old man. He saw the dark sweep of the buffalo robe as it was flung over the head of Spotted Antelope.

The keepers of the entrance stood back, opening the way to the young man, their eyes on the ground. He stepped out into the blinding brightness of the morning; and shrilling in his ears, he heard the outcry of the children and the women as they realized that the tribe had lost a warrior and gained a lasting shame. He went on rapidly, his head fallen.

Once again he heard lifted a single voice of woe. He knew that that was the cry of Bitter Root, his foster-mother.

The eyes of the world were killing him, it seemed, and he began to run. A dog seemed to think it a game, and bounded at his heels, frolicking about him. He came to his father's lodge, flung open the entrance, and hurled himself on the ground. Great sobs began to work in his body, swelling his breast, thrusting into his throat; but not a sound could reach his lips.

CHAPTER 6

A STEP sounded and paused beside him. Someone crouched by his body. A hand lay on his shoulder, and the voice of Standing Bull said:

"It is I, brother!"

That last word pierced Red Hawk's heart. He groaned. "I am no longer your brother. I pour shame on all who are near me; I pour it out as the night pours darkness."

"Oh, my friend," said the warrior, "the hand that strikes you, strikes me. The blow that hangs over you, hangs over me. The flesh is farther from the bone than you are from my heart."

Such grief came over Red Hawk that he wondered why the sobbing could not reach his mouth or why the tears did not rush into his eyes. He lay still, with his fingers buried in his hair.

A woman's voice of lament came out of the distance, approached them, swelled suddenly through the lodge as Bitter Root entered and flung herself down by the fire. She had already torn off her clothes until she was naked to the waist. Now, with a long skinning knife, she chopped her gray hair short; she began to gash her legs, her arms, her breast, snatching up ashes from the edge of the fire and pouring them over her head. And all the time she rocked herself back and forth with a double cry of monotonous lament.

Red Hawk got to his hands and knees and crawled to her. He held out his arms in supplication. He found his voice, to speak, but her eyes were filled with madness and unknowing.

Spotted Antelope entered, sat on the ground, and covered his head with his robe.

Then Standing Bull touched the shoulder of his friend once more. "Come!" he said.

Red Hawk stood up and followed the brave out of the lodge. In the distance he could hear the yelling of the women and children as some one of the martyred sufferers from the medicine lodge was dragged behind the heels of a running horse.

"I must die," said Red Hawk. "There is no more life for me. I cannot crouch among the women. I cannot carry burdens and chop wood and build fires and cook like a squaw. I must die!"

"This is only one day, and even this day has not ended," said Standing Bull. "Here is the lodge of Lazy Wolf. Ask him what you should do. The girl is weeping. Do you hear?"

"She knows that I am a coward. Last night when she saw me I was almost a man. Now I am nothing! How can I go inside?"

At that moment the entrance flap was pushed back by Lazy Wolf. He was wearing his spectacles, so that his round, hairy face looked more than ever owlish; and he had between his teeth one of the short-stemmed pipes that white men use.

He stood aside and waved them in. Red Hawk entered the lodge, white and brilliant with the strong morning light of the sun. Blue Bird, throwing a light deerskin over her head, rose from a willow bed and slipped out through the entrance, shrouded and bowed like an old woman. But the face of Lazy Wolf was calm, as he sat down with his guests.

Standing Bull took out a pipe, filled and lighted it with ceremony, blew smoke to the ground, to the Listeners Above, to the four quarters of the world.

"Let all the world of men and spirits know that this man is still my brother!" he said, and passed the pipe to Lazy Wolf.

The older of the two white men smiled as he puffed in a similar ceremonious manner. "My lad," said he, "let the spirits and all the men of the world know that I, also, am still your friend. And why not? No white man with his wits about him would go through the butchery of the medicine lodge. Your heart is not as red as you think, my son. However, it's true that life from now on will be hell for you in this camp—for a time, at least. The thing for you to do is to take a horse and ride across the hills and across the plains until you come to some town of the whites. They'll never think a whit less of you because you've not collected a set of scars."

"Leave my people!" cried Red Hawk. "If I leave them, it will mean a death in every day of my life. When the sun rises, it will find me among the whites, who are weak and foolish; who lie and cheat; who murder the Cheyennes with tricks and cunning and black evil—and who do not know anything great or good!"

"They make the rifles which the Cheyennes shoot with," said Lazy Wolf, calmly, "and the knives which the Indians use, the blankets they want, the bright cloth, the beads, the axes and hatchets. They bring the tea and the sugar. Except for his horses and robes, what is the wealth of a Cheyenne except the things that the traders bring to him from the whites?"

"The work of squaws!" said Red Hawk. He raised his head and one hand, in a fine gesture of disdain. "They are a people without strength. Their ugly faces and bodies are the color of the bellies of fish. Ah, Lazy Wolf, why do you tell me to go among them? Why should I not die quickly among my people rather than go among the strangers like them?"

Lazy Wolf turned to the warrior. "Talk to him," he said, briefly.

Standing Bull nodded. He stood up by the center-pole, gathered his robe about him.

"I have no years," he said. "I have not sat among the old men and heard their wisdom. I can only say to my brother that nothing but the strong sun keeps his skin dark, and that since his blood is white, perhaps he will be happy among the white men. I shall follow you as far as you go, and never leave you till you have reached a white camp.

And once I have learned the trail to your new people, nothing but death can keep me from coming in a summer, or over the snow, to look into the face of my brother."

Red Hawk bowed his head.

"That," said Lazy Wolf, "is a very true, sensible and knowing sort of speech. Standing Bull, you are a fellow of promise. You have a brain—with a tongue hitched to it—and I want to see you in my tepee more often. Now then, Red Hawk, make up your mind. Are you going to stay on like a dog in the Cheyenne camp? Are you going to cut your throat like a fool and turn yourself into carrion for the buzzards to eat? Or are you going back to *your own* people?"

Red Hawk caught the hand of Lazy Wolf with a sudden gesture. "Tell me!" he said. "And you, Standing Bull, tell me. Could I ever return?"

"You could," said Lazy Wolf instantly.

"There are some among us who will always be waiting," said Standing Bull.

Red Hawk felt that something in him was dying; he knew a sorrow so great that his heart grew small under the weight of it. So he sat in silence, feeling now and again the glance of Lazy Wolf.

At last the host said, "Now is the time to go, while all the rest are yet at the blood sacrifice. Get your best horse."

Red Hawk rose like a man in a dream, saddled a tough little gray stallion, which was his best horse, and returned to the tepee of Lazy Wolf. Standing Bull, with a saddled pony, was already waiting for him.

Then from the medicine lodge he saw the great war chief of the tribe come suddenly towards them, striding rapidly. There was hardly a red Indian of the plains more famous than Dull Hatchet, and now that he was dressed in full regalia for the ceremony of the medicine lodge, he seemed to Red Hawk the most magnificent of figures.

The war chief's imposing headdress of stained eagle-feathers swept from his head and trailed on the ground behind him, and at least a score of those feathers were tied at the tips with the hairs that were the sign of many grand coups.

That headdress alone overwhelmed the eye and the mind of Red Hawk; but everything about the person of Dull Hatchet was extraordinary, from the necklace of a hundred grizzly bear claws to the tassels of ermine tails that hung from a hundred places.

There were other details which enchanted the eye of Red Hawk to such a degree that in the glory of his war chief he almost forgot his disgrace. He brooded on the stern face of the hero, which was gashed across one cheek by a deep scar. There were plenty of other battle marks on the body of the old warrior; but strange to say, this mark which helped to make him so terrible of aspect was the result of a bullet fired at him by a woman. How weak his medicine must have been on that day, thought Red Hawk!

Then he heard Dull Hatchet saying, grimly:

"One good deed is not enough to fill a life. Brave men have been forgotten, Standing Bull. And a brave is known not by the wife we find in his tepee, but by the friends who pass through the entrance flap. Standing Bull, you are looked for in the medicine lodge. Return!"

He half turned as he said this, pointing his lance toward the distant lodge. But to the amazement of Red Hawk, his friend made not the least move to obey his war leader! Such a thing was unheard of.

A war chief of the Cheyennes, it is true, seldom gives commands when he is in camp; but once his voice is lifted, it is hardly second in authority to that of the supreme chief, or the head medicine man and wizard of the tribe.

Still young Standing Bull had not moved, though Red Hawk was gasping, "Go!—Go quickly! I am nothing, brother!—Go quickly before he is angry!"

It was plain that Standing Bull was in the greatest of anguish, for nothing could be a larger handicap to the career of a rising young brave than hostility on the part of his war chief. Honorable missions would be withheld from him, and his name would be omitted from important war-parties. With a gesture, the chief was able to sweep almost any brave into obscurity.

The command had been given and it would not be repeated; the face of the great leader was already darkened before Standing Bull managed to say:

"You have been a father to me on the war trail; you have been a shield to turn bullets from me; and you have been a knife in my hand. But I have heard old men say that a friend is more than a breath in the nostrils."

The delay might have prepared the chief in part; nevertheless Dull Hatchet was shocked by these last words. The long lance shuddered in his grasp as he turned gradually; then the blood rushed into his face and seemed to stain his eyes as they kept their savage hold on Standing Bull to the last instant.

When the back of the war leader had been turned, Red Hawk caught the arm of his friend and shook it. "Go after him!" he whispered. "Walk at his side. Quickly! Tell him that a darkness fell over your mind, and that now you see clearly again. Go back with him or your life will be sad; and whenever you think of me you will groan and cover your head."

He finished the last words in a weak voice, for already Standing Bull was drawing himself up, composing his face, gathering his strength in quietness as an Indian will do when his mind is irrevocably fixed on some dangerous goal.

Lazy Wolf, who stood behind them, said calmly, "Standing Bull, if you're riding with him, do you know the shortest way to one of the camps of the white men?"

"No," said the brave.

Lazy Wolf sat on his heels, and in Indian fashion he drew a trail-map on the ground, describing the marks as he made them.

Here he indicated a lone tree, there a flat-headed mesa, now an empty draw, then a river which could be forded at a certain place. And as he made the design, Standing Bull, watching intently, copied it with his own finger in the dust. He would not forget. Cheyennes have traveled safely over a thousand miles of unknown country with no better guidance.

"And here," concluded Lazy Wolf, "you come to the Witherell Creek. Follow down it until you reach the hills, and inside the hills you'll come to the town of Witherell itself."

He stood up and took the hand of Red Hawk.

"When at last you come to your own white people," he said, "remember that although they're new to you, you can learn to taste life as they taste it. Be quiet. Use your eyes. Then a great many things will come to you easily that you could never win by fighting."

He held Red Hawk's hand as they walked to the edge of the village, and even went with them for a few paces beyond the outmost circle of lodges. Then he stopped.

That stopping wrenched at the heart of Red Hawk. "I must go back," he said, breathing deep. "I must go back to say farewell to my father and mother."

"Your mother is still howling and your father has blinded himself," answered Lazy Wolf. "I'll tell them that you've gone, and say why you didn't wait to speak to them. I'll give them farewell gifts, also. Go quickly—good-bye, Red Hawk!"

Lazy Wolf turned away, with this final remark, and marched straight back among the lodges. Once he hesitated; then continued on his way.

Red Hawk groaned, "It is true. They no longer have a son. In their lodge I am dead. Tomorrow I shall have been a ghost for a hundred years."

CHAPTER 7

THREE things of importance, never to be forgotten, were seen by Red Hawk on the way to the town of Witherell from the Black Hills. First, as he rode with Standing Bull down the narrow ravine of the first stream that watered the camp, he looked up by chance and saw what seemed to him, at first, a white rock on the verge of the bluff, high above him.

But rocks cannot move, and after a moment he realized that it was the Blue Bird in the shining newness of her doeskin dress.

He stared at her until he saw her make a gesture with both hands; then he dropped his head and galloped the gray stallion swiftly down the ravine, far out of sight of the girl. Yet afterwards she remained in his mind so clearly that often he wished he had last seen her in shadow rather than in sunshine, so that she would not gleam so in his memory, coming to him out of a distance.

On the third day, as they voyaged over the northern

plains, a herd of wild horses, smaller than grains of dust on the palm of that gigantic hand, moved out of the eastern horizon and poured at a gallop closer and closer, until Red Hawk saw a thing that glistened like the sharpened point of a lance.

He halted his gray stallion. He threw up his arms and shouted, "Look, Standing Bull! It is the White Horse! It is the White Horse!"

Standing Bull drew close to him. They leaned from their saddles a little towards one another. The greatness of their excitement surrounded them like fear.

The herd swept nearer, still resembling a dark lance head with a shining point, until at last they had a nearer view of the White Horse than ever a Cheyenne had had. They were close enough to see the mark of darkness between the eyes, and how all four legs were stockinged at least fetlock high with black silk. All the rest of him was purest white.

He came right on at them, as though he led home a charge; but angling suddenly, he went off at full gallop, his mane and tail blown like feathers by his speed. They watched him marshal his little host away, rounding to the rear of the herd to drive up the laggards with the ringing bugle call of his neigh. And afterwards the two men looked for a long time on one another with eyes made dull by the pain of a hopeless desire.

The White Horse was new to fame. He had led herds across the plains and up into the mountain valleys for only two seasons. But already Comanches in the south, Pawnees and Blackfeet to the west, the Dakotas to the north, and the riders of the Cheyennes had all melted away the best of their horseflesh in the vain effort to catch the stallion.

That was why the two young Cheyennes sat in their saddles quietly and made no effort now to pursue. Then Standing Bull lifted a hand towards the sky; and Red Hawk

39

knew that he could name with ease the subject of the warrior's silent prayer.

They were less than a day from the end of their journey when they came to the third great milestone of the expedition. Riding down the bank of Witherell Creek, they came to the ruins of a sod house which many winters had beaten and melted into a sodden heap out of which only a few rotten poles were thrusting. More poles, sticking up through the grass, vaguely indicated what had once been a fenced inclosure. It was by no means an unusual sight, for the prairie was daubed here and there by the dim ruins of the houses of white settlers. This site, however, was more particularly marked by a large white stone, evidently quarried at a distance and brought here at the cost of a great effort, for it was far too ponderous for Red Hawk to budge, no matter how he strained at it.

He had dismounted because out of this obscure place something spoke to him. Standing Bull stood by with folded arms and watched. It was he, however, who called the attention of Red Hawk to what he called the "medicine pictures" on the face of that stone. Then Red Hawk, who had been taught elementary reading by Lazy Wolf, made out the chiseled letters, pointing them out with his fingers and gradually grouping them into the sound of syllables, until the words were complete.

"Kate Sabin lies here, killed by the murdering Cheyennes of Dull Hatchet."

Red Hawk sprang to his feet. "Wind Walker!" he cried.

The name made even Standing Bull leap aside as though to dodge a lance thrust from behind.

"Wind Walker!" repeated Red Hawk. "This is the grave of his squaw. This is where he buried the woman for whose sake he is still hunting the Cheyennes. For this is how they bury a squaw or a brave—in the dark and the wet and the

40

cold of the earth instead of leaving them wrapped on a platform where the sun can shine on them and the wind blow on them."

He fell into such a long pause that his friend at last said gently, "What is rising in you? Your throat works. Shall we sing a chant?"

Gradually Red Hawk extended his left arm.

"There should be corn-land yonder!" he said suddenly.

Standing Bull went instantly to the indicated place.

"There is nothing here," he said, trailing his moccasins over the ground to feel the face of it through the grass. "Ha! Now I find some small bumps—now others. And in rows, do you see? Yes, this must have been corn-land, long ago."

He came back and looked into the dreamy face of Red Hawk. "This is a strange thing, brother!" he said in an awed voice. "When your eyes look inside of you, what do they see?"

"Nothing!" said Red Hawk. "Only shadows and dimly moving things. But I can hear something."

"What do you hear?" asked the warrior.

"A voice that says a thing which has no meaning. Besides, it is a woman's voice! Standing Bull, is it the voice of the buried squaw? It is sounding deeply, inside me."

"What is the sound?"

"There is no meaning to it," said Red Hawk. "But she calls in me—'Rusty.'"

"That is a word in the speech of the white men. It is not Cheyenne," suggested Standing Bull.

"It is a word of the whites," agreed Red Hawk.

"This is a dangerous thing," said Standing Bull, very gravely. "When ghosts speak out of the ground, old men say that death is near to us."

"Ride on down the creek. I must stay here for a little

41

time," answered Red Hawk. "Either this inside me is the voice of a ghost, or the ghost of a memory, and how could I remember a thing which has never been? If it is a ghost, it is a friendly one."

"Why do you say so?" asked Standing Bull.

Red Hawk answered, "Because I feel now a sorrowful happiness—like that which I feel when I think of the lodge of my father, now that I am far away from it. It is happiness to remember, and it is grief to know that it is lost to me. Ride down the creek, my brother. Leave me alone here, and I shall follow soon."

But he did not follow quickly, according to his promise. Instead, he remained for long hours, wrapped in his buffalo robe, seated cross-legged beside the white stone of the grave. Sometimes he put out his hand and touched it, hot as it was with the sun; and it seemed to him like the touch of flesh. But all the while, images were rising up in his mind like bubbles in a dark fountain, so that he could never see their faces—headless ghosts. At last he stood up and climbed again into the saddle.

Standing Bull asked no questions, for he saw in the face of his friend a thing that was beyond speech.

It was because of this delay that they did not pass through the hills into view of Witherell until the sunset had dwindled to a smudge.

As they paused in the dark throat of the little valley and looked down on the lights of the town that lay in the hollow, it seemed to Red Hawk that he was looking through dim water, at strange spots of sunlight on the bottom of a stream. There was no moon.

They stood in silence so long that he could mark the up-drift of the stars above the eastern hills.

Standing Bull said, "I go back to the tribe now; and you go forward to your people. I shall come again."

42

CHAPTER 8

WHAT Red Hawk said to his friend he could never remember, though he would not forget to his death the sound of the hoofs of Standing Bull's horse as it went back through the pass.

Then he saw the last of the sunset had died out to a muddy yellow, while the night, like a shadow cast upward from the ground, rose and closed over him in a cold flood. Each light before him meant a lodge, he supposed, and to one of them he would have to go for shelter. As for the choice among them, it must be left to his "medicine." So he made medicine, simply by picking up a small portion of dust from the trail and blowing on it until only the little pebbles remained in the palm of his hand. With the cautious tips of his fingers he counted four grains of rock; therefore he would pass four lights, and at the fifth he would try to enter.

He rode on down the trail until he came to an opening that clove straight through the camp of the white men. The lights, he now observed, shone very clearly out of the sides of the lodges, and out of their faces, but he could not see the dancing, wavering glow of flames.

He counted one light on the left and three on the right, and straightway turned towards the next light on the left. A wooden fence stopped him, so that he was forced to dismount. He started to explore the place on foot, leaving the gray stallion tethered to the fence.

All was strange. Apparently there were no scouts abroad.

43

Though a dog barked now and again, there was no prowling crowd of them, such as continually washed across an Indian camp.

Against the stars, he studied the outlines of the lodge which was before him. In compass, he calculated, it might be large enough to accommodate a hundred or more men around the sides; yet out of its immensity came only a small drifting current of noises from the rear—chiefly the voices of talking women, with the deeper tones of a man sounding through at intervals.

He leaped the fence and landed on soft cultivated ground. He found a hard path to the right, covered with masses of small stones, the sharp edges of which he could feel through his moccasins. To walk silently over such a surface was almost impossible.

Out of the dullness of starshine before him rose steps which the touch of his hand proved to be of wood levelled wonderfully smooth; and with that it began to be more apparent to him that the medicine of the white man was indeed strong. These wooden steps were inclined to make groaning noises, so that it required all of five minutes for him to mount them in the necessary silence.

To his left the light shone through a square hole in the wall, and as he stood before the opening he looked into a mystery indeed! What he saw was a chamber of about the size, say, of an eight-skin lodge—but the place was not rounded; it was square! At one side stood a solid mass of black iron, as high as his breast-bone, with a tube of black rising from the top and vanishing through the roof.

Around the walls were what appeared to be books, for they were very like the volume owned by Lazy Wolf; but the brain of Red Hawk ached when he considered the incalculable swarms of words that must be required to fill them.

The floor, strange to say, was not of beaten earth, but of wood smoothed over, and polished with brown paint. How long would it take a man to hew down logs to such a level, and then polish them, one by one? But in the center of the room, on a small raised floor of wood which was supported by four legs, stood the chief miracle of all—a small flame that burned inside a gleaming transparent cylinder, larger at the bottom than at the top. Most mysterious of all was the nature of the flame itself. It neither leaped nor shrank. It seemed to spring, moreover, out of nothingness!

When Red Hawk had considered this mighty marvel for a time, he moved forward to lean through the hole in the wall of the lodge and observe what was still hidden from him. But his nose struck in the invisible air something as cold as ice, and as hard.

He lurched back. Then, with the tips of his fingers, very cautiously, he examined the surface of this marvel which was something and yet was nothing. It was in fact, a sort of dry ice, and it permitted the eye to glance unimpeded into the interior of the lodge. Awe came upon Red Hawk. He felt that he was staring at a temple, and that this was a sacred fire which through the dreadful magic of the white man, fed upon the thin air instead of any substance.

When his mind had tasted these immensities for some time, he left the front of this great, square, wooden lodge, and went to the rear. He was now closer to the voices, and, again advancing with infinite caution up the wooden steps, he came closer to the white magicians.

Again the light streamed upon him, through another partition of the dry ice, emanating from just such a flame, enclosed in a similar crystal tube. What manner of people were these who could keep in a single lodge two marvels, each of which was enough to make the fame of a great medicine man? He could not look into their faces at once. Instead, he glanced towards a corner where stood another mass of black iron. Out of this iron came flickerings of yellow fire and the noise of shuddering flames.

Now he was able to see that two women and a man sat about the four-legged structure which supported the steady flame in the crystal tube. They were not worshiping. No, they were talking and laughing, their pale faces wrinkling and opening with mirth as though their bellies had been filled after long fasting. For this there was small cause of wonder, since it was apparently a mighty feast! Not out of wooden bowls with horn spoons did they feed; they ate from rounded, flat stones, very white and shining.

Other marvels appeared on that lighted altar, and not the least were seven knives! To be sure the handles of them were absurdly small, yet they were apparently steel of good quality.

Then it could be noted that these people sat on stools which had backs to them, against which they leaned like mighty enchanters, secure in the presence of their magic fire. And last of all, Red Hawk observed their faces; and he felt the difference between the whites and the Cheyennes more than ever he had when he looked at the sun-browned traders whom he had seen in the camp.

The face of the man was sharp below the eyes; the eyes themselves were large, well opened, calm, with the shadow of thought constantly on them. But the forehead rose lofty, wide, and shining.

The squaw was not very different. In spite of the fact that they seemed now to be carelessly feasting upon at least six kinds of food, it was apparent that the man and the older woman fasted often, for she was as lean of feature as the master of the lodge. Her hair was gray; her eyes were misty blue; from the thinness of her shoulders it was plain

46

that she would be of small use in shifting camp or carrying water or fleshing hides! Yet she looked about with the calm demeanor of the young and favorite squaw of a mighty chief.

Last of all Red Hawk looked at the girl, though he had been aware of her from the first, as one is aware of distant music, no matter where the eyes and mind may be. She fitted into the days of his life like a blue lake among the iron mountains. The light remained in her hair, and he could not tell whether he wished to follow the motion of her hands or the brown beauty of her face. Unlike the others, it was plain that the sun loved her and dwelt much on her.

She put back her head in laughter, at this moment; and her mirth tilted her from side to side a little. Then her eyes suddenly rested on the window where Red Hawk stood.

The laughter vanished. She sprang up with a scream, pointing.

The two other heads turned. The other woman cried out, also. As Red Hawk stepped back, he heard a trampling of hasty feet and the older woman's voice crying:

"Don't go out, Richard!"

"Stuff and nonsense!" said the man, and cast the door open. The shaft of light flashed along the barrel of the rifle which the man held, and then struck full on his form.

Red Hawk drew himself up slowly. One should always move gently when the guns are pointed. Lifting his hands, he gathered his dignity into his voice, saying:

"How!"

"It's a friendly redskin," said the white man.

"There's no such thing!" cried his squaw from the inside of the lodge.

"Do you speak English? What you want?" asked the man.

"I speak English," said Red Hawk. "I come from the

47

Black Hills to live among the white men, because my skin is also white."

"The devil it is!" said the other. "Come inside."

He stood back, making a gesture of invitation which Red Hawk accepted, stepping lightly over the threshold. The two women were in a corner; the mother with a hand thrown up across her face, ready to shield her eyes from the sight of a monstrosity; the girl all eyes with fear, but with her chin thrusting out in a determined way. She held a big revolver in both hands.

Red Hawk, having printed their faces on his mind, looked down at the floor.

"He can't stay here," said the squaw. "I won't have him under the same roof with us. We'd wake up to find the place in flames. I don't know what you're thinking of, Richard Lester!"

"I haven't said that I'm thinking of it," said Lester. "He speaks English, my dear, so ask him to sit down. Take this chair, my friend. Maisry, set a new place at the table. Put the meat and the beans back into the oven to heat, and make some more coffee."

It was a hospitable speech, and the voice was warm and kindly, with more delicacy of inflection than Red Hawk ever had heard from a human throat.

The older woman suddenly cried out, "Merciful heaven, Richard! It's true! His skin is white—or almost white. Make him sit down. He must have been stolen away from his family by the red devils! What is your name, young man? Were the members of your family murdered?"

"Hush, Martha!" said Richard Lester. "Let him take his breath."

The eye of Red Hawk swung to the side to watch the girl open a door in the hot iron monster and put meat and a platter of beans inside it. Then he answered:

"My father is Spotted Antelope, a brave man who has

taken five scalps, two of them from white men. He has counted coup of three living men, and on twelve dead ones. My mother is Bitter Root. She has been a medicine lodge woman; her hands are never still all day long, and—"

"Murder!" cried the white squaw. "Five scalps! And two from white men—"

"Martha," said Richard Lester, "if your tongue *must* keep joggling along, I'll have to ask you to leave the room. This man is our guest, and he understands every word you speak! My friend, will you sit down?"

He pushed forward, again, one of the stools with the high backs; but Red Hawk, unfamiliar with this medicine, threw back from his naked shoulders his buffalo robe and squatted crosslegged on the floor.

"You father is a white man who joined the Indians?" said Lester. "Is that it?"

"My father is red. He is Cheyenne, and his name is Spotted Antelope."

"Ah!" said Lester, his voice hard. "And he has a white squaw, then?"

"My mother is also red," said Red Hawk. "Her name is Bitter Root, and—"

"But if both your parents are red, how does it come that your skin is white?" asked Lester.

Red Hawk answered, "My father is Spotted Antelope. My mother is Bitter Root. That is all I know."

"He was taken as a child. He doesn't remember," said the girl. "And all of these questions will embarrass him. Offer him something to smoke. That's the best way."

"It is," said Lester. "Well—are you comfortable on that cold floor, my friend? And what is your name?"

"My name is Red Hawk. The floor is as warm to me as piled buffalo robes, because the voice of my white friend is kind."

"Thank you," said Lester. "My name is Richard Lester."

Red Hawk stood up.

"This is my wife; this is my daughter, Maisry," Lester continued.

Red Hawk looked at them both, and then sat down again on the floor. Lester took a chair opposite him.

"So you've left the Cheyennes and you've come to live with the whites?" said Richard Lester. "And what will you do? What work will you undertake?"

"I shall join some chief," said Red Hawk, "and follow him on the war path and take scalps wherever I can."

"Good heavens!" cried Martha Lester.

"Hush, my dear!" said the husband. "But listen to me, Red Hawk. The people of this town don't have chiefs, and they don't ride on the war path. All that we want is peace; and we work to make the town grow and the farm lands extend farther and farther through the hills. Do you understand?"

The mind of Red Hawk grasped vainly at this picture. "I have heard that white men work like squaws," he said. "Do you use a hoe in the fields?"

"I work with books," said Lester. "I am a lawyer. That is to say, when two men quarrel, I try to make peace between them—or else I try to prove that one is right and the other wrong. For that they give me money."

"A peacemaker," said Red Hawk, "is better in a camp than a great war chief on a man-trail."

"But all of us," said Lester, "work in some way. What sort of work would you like to do?"

"What *could* he do?" asked Mrs. Lester. "Now there's Sam Calkins, the blacksmith. He's lacking an apprentice. That would be a place for him. He looks strong enough."

"Sam Calkins," said the girl, opening the oven door and taking out the platter that held the joint, "is a great, surly brute!"

50

"All the better taskmaster for a red-handed—" began Mrs. Lester.

"Hush, Martha!" said Richard Lester. "If there's a place open with Calkins, it might serve to give Red Hawk his start; he wouldn't have to stay with Calkins if he didn't want to. In the meantime, I can look around and try to find something worth while for him to do. Put the platter down on the floor before our guest, Maisry."

The girl, accordingly, placed the big dish in front of Red Hawk, and with it a small plate, a knife, a fork, a spoon, a dish of baked beans, some bread on another plate, and a steaming cup of coffee.

"Sugar?" she asked, offering a bowl of it, with a spoon held tentatively above it.

"Good!" cried Red Hawk, his mouth watering.

Taking the bowl, he poured a large quantity of that precious sweet stuff into his mouth and began to champ it noisily. There was a gasping cry of disgust from Mrs. Lester; but in the ecstasy of his pleasure, Red Hawk's dim eyes were unable to discover the cause of her exclamation. In a few mouthfuls, he had finished the sugar, and began to clear his throat, which had been a little rasped. His mouth being wet to the chin, he dried it on his forearm.

"I'm leaving the room! I can't stand it!" said Mrs. Lester. "A more disgusting—" Then she broke off to add, "Maisry, what in heaven's name is the matter with you? Get up off that floor!"

For Maisry, at this point, had actually sat down cross-legged, opposite to Red Hark. He smiled and nodded to her, grateful for this company of his own level, as it were. And the girl said: "You know, Mother, we want him to feel at home."

"Richard Lester, order your child to get up off that floor!" cried the mother.

"I can't do it, Martha," said the lawyer. "Maisry is right. I ought to do the same thing, I suppose, but I'm afraid of rheumatism, and if—"

His voice died away as Red Hawk took the bone of the meat in both hands, by the joints, and commenced to rip away the flesh with his strong teeth. It was so tender that it came away in large fragments, which he gathered into his mouth with vigorous use of his lips and tongue. Presently the bone was stripped white and gleaming. The beans received his next attention, and resting the edge of the bowl between his chin and his lower lip, he took the spoon in a comfortable grip and began to shovel. He closed his eyes, and presently the spoon scraped on the bottom of the bowl.

At this, he put down the bowl and tried the coffee; but since it was unsweetened and still very hot, he squirted out on the floor the half-mouthful which he tried. After that, he fitted his pipe together and filled it for a smoke.

The girl set about mopping up the coffee-spot with a wet rag, while her father sat by rubbing his chin. Mrs. Lester had left the room.

A spirit of peace came over Red Hawk as he inhaled the tobacco fumes deeply. Being moved to sing, he parted his lips, swayed a little from side to side to keep the rhythm and began his song, drawling out the monotony of it, occasionally lifting his voice to a yelp, till in the strength of his pleasure he could see only the face of the girl.

When he had finished she said to him: "What is your song about, Red Hawk?"

"I am glad that you ask me," said he. "This is what it says in white words, without singing: 'Old winter, you are gone from me. The new grass is rising through the brown. There's plenty of back-fat in the pot, stewing with buffalo tongues. My belly is full and my heart is comforted. Smoke fills me with happiness. Then why will not sleep come to me? Because, when I close my eyes, I see my love like a place of flowers in the middle of a great plain.' "

He made a gesture towards the girl, palm out.

"That is for you," he said.

Her eyes were pleased, and perfectly calm. She smiled straight at him. "Thank you," she said.

"It's growing late," said Richard Lester suddenly. "I'll show you a bed where you may sleep, Red Hawk. And in the morning I'll see the blacksmith and try to get him to let you work for him—at least for a while."

"Do you mean that I must work with my hands?" said Red Hawk.

He looked down at his palms, and moved his fingers.

"Either with your hands or with your wits," said Richard Lester. "And until you've learned the ways of the whites, you'd better depend on your hands. It's a painful medicine, but a good one."

He stood up from the chair. Red Hawk rose, also. He was greatly contented, for the white chief had spoken to him with much kindness. If among the whites there were such men, if among the whites there were such girls as this, if the lodges were filled with such miracles of crystal and fire and comfort, was not life at least possible?

"Good-night," said the girl.

"May the night be good to you, also," said Red Hawk. "May kind voices speak in your dreams!"

He followed his host down a narrow hall and into a small chamber that contained, in one corner, a bed raised on four legs and covered with blankets.

"Sleep well," said Richard Lester, "and good-night, Red Hawk."

"May all the white tribes honor you!" said Red Hawk, with emotion.

But when he was left alone it seemed to him that the

muffled voices which spoke in other parts of the place were stealing towards him; and when he laid himself on the bed there was a stirring and a thin creaking of metal under it.

Then he remembered his horse. He got up, took his buffalo robe, and spent many long minutes before he could get out of the place without bringing a creak from a single board underfoot. When he leaped the fence the gray stallion began to whinny, but he caught it by the nostrils and held on until the tremor of effort ceased.

Afterwards he found a bit of grass not far from the lodge of Richard Lester, so he stripped off the saddle, hobbled the horse, gave the blanket a single twist around his body and lay down, as it were, in the middle of a camp of enemies.

But before sleep came he grasped in his right hand the little green beetle, of stone, with the hawk engraved upon it, which hung from about his neck.

"Beetle," he said softly, "you have opened your wings and carried me a great distance. You have taken me into a good land. My belly is full. The same stars shine on me as on the Cheyennes. So why does my heart ache so?"

Then he slept.

CHAPTER 9

ALL was still black when he awakened. Standing up, he saw the pale hand of day behind the hills, blackening them, and so he saddled the gray and rode up the side of a hill. It was still too dark for him to distinguish features in the valley beneath him, therefore he was guided to water by the sound of its running. In the cool wind of dawn he stripped, washed with icy water, and pulled on his clothes again.

By this time the first color was beginning and the trees along the tops of the hills were awash with flame. At last he could see the camp in the hollow clearly.

As it first grew on his eye out of the darkness he refused to credit his senses, for one beyond the other he saw big huddling shapes, each larger than a medicine lodge. He discovered that there were lodges by twenties and twenties and twenties, many of them far larger than that of Richard Lester. Were they all chiefs, then? Were they all great?

Riding down to the lodge of his white friend, he saw a strange matter. The girl was in a fenced enclosure behind the house, milking a cow that closed its eyes in dull content and chewed its cud with a wagging jaw. This was very proper. But at a pile of wood that had already been cut into lengths, the great chief, Richard Lester, the peacemaker and chief, was wielding an axe and splitting the logs.

Red Hawk regarded this marvel with a dropping jaw. It was true that the squaw seemed small for such labor; but then why did not the chief take a second wife into his lodge—a young strong woman, able to hew and carry?

He put his horse into a closed pasture and came towards the house. Smoke was spouting from the top of it. An odor of food crept out to him.

Then Richard Lester hailed him, cheerfully. The girl came in with a bucket half filled with milk, frothing and slopping in the pail. The back door of the lodge opened, and the sharp voice of Mrs. Lester called out that breakfast was ready.

It was a meal made memorable by Red Hawk's initiation to flapjacks and syrup, and by the fact that he sat for the first time in a chair. He was confused by the explanations which his few questions brought upon him. The making of porcelain; the weaving of cloth; mills that sawed and planed wood; and, above all, the mystery of the oil lamp was made clear to him.

After breakfast, Richard Lester gave him a blue woolen shirt and strongly urged that he should have his hair cut off.

"Everything that makes you strange to the people of the town," said Lester, "will help to keep you at a distance. I have some old clothes. Perhaps even my shoes will fit you. If you are to live among us, you ought to take up all our ways."

Red Hawk looked from his skin-fitted leggings to the clumsiness of the trousers; from his supple moccasins to the unwieldy leather shoes. He shook his head.

"If I change so much," he answered, "it would be as though I wore a new face. My Cheyenne brothers would never know me. But the shirt is very good. It makes me half a white man, at once."

So he put it on, letting the tails of it fall down outside his leggings, of course. Over the shirt he threw his robe, and in that garb he left the house of Richard Lester, accompanied by his host. Mrs. Lester peered at them from a window, but the girl went on to the gate of the garden and shook hands with Red Hawk.

"This is his first day of school," she said to her father. "Be good to him!"

"It is a woman of understanding who makes happiness in the tepee," remarked Red Hawk, as they went down the street. "But why does she speak of school?"

"Because there's a great deal for you to learn," said the lawyer. "Most of it will be hard, simply because it is new. And here come the boys to plague you. Boys have no manners, and they'll laugh at anything new."

It seemed as though all the youngsters in the town had been lurking in wait to fall on the stranger, for now they

56

poured out into the street and made a whirling pool around Red Hawk. They shouted, they leaped, they pointed deriding fingers at him, but he stepped on with unseeing eyes.

So they came to the small square which made the center of the town of Witherell, and there Red Hawk saw a figure from the plains that made his heart jump. He was of the type of those wild white men who took scalps as readily as the Indians, but without any Indian ceremonies. Dressed in deerskins so grease-stained and time-polished that they looked like varnished leather, on his head he wore a flopping hat of black felt, with his hair pouring from under it in tangled strings, as far as his shoulders.

The plainsman sat on a mustang with a braided mane, and across the pommel of the saddle balanced one of those long-barreled, old-fashioned rifles which, in certain hands, seemed unable to miss.

When the trapper saw the Indian figure of Red Hawk, he shifted his rifle suddenly to the ready and remained with it so, on guard.

He was not the only one to mark the howling mob of boys and the strange figure in the center of the cluster, for there were many other men opening for the day the stores and small shops and saloons that surrounded the square. All of them paused to stare at Red Hawk. It was true that Indians were often seen in Witherell, but "white" Indians very seldom.

Now Lester cut straight across the square towards a low shed in front of which half a dozen horses were hitched at a long rack.

From the wide-open doors of the place there rolled an atmosphere of blue smoke, while the clangor of iron on iron rang from it.

"This is Sam Calkins's blacksmith shop," said Lester. "He's a big, rough fellow, full of fight; but I believe he's

57

honest enough—and he loves his work. I'm going to ask him if he can give you a place.

"Just wait a moment while I talk to him."

Red Hawk, at the side of the double door, looked in upon new marvels. Compared with them, even Lester's house was nothing. For along the walls hung tools of iron or of bright steel, in shapes so many and strange that the imagination of a medicine man would have been strained to conceive them. In a corner, with a metal hood stretched over it to collect most of the smoke, there was a large box filled with fire. Beside the box, Red Hawk saw, was a contrivance of leather, with a long wooden handle which was worked up and down by the blacksmith. At every downstroke it made a wheezing sound, and the yellow flame of the fire turned into a shooting blue.

With a long-handled tool of iron, the smith now lifted out of the fire a mass that glowed almost white, and sent off a constant shower of sparks.

Sam Calkins was a six-foot giant, not that six feet made a man look tall on the plains, but because nature had piled on him a load of muscle and fat that had bowed his legs and made him walk with a waddle. About him there was no weak part. Everywhere was an immensity of bone and flesh; and the very legs which appeared hardly able to bear up the bulk of his body were twice the normal size.

He had not yet given any answer to Lester's words, nor any sign that he had so much as heard him speak. Now he stepped with the knot of iron to the ponderous square of black metal which was nailed in place on the round section of a log. With his tongs in the left hand, he managed the iron; with his right hand he wielded a twelve-pound hammer, beating the lump of iron into shape.

Presently he took it back to the fire, and again began to lean his weight rhythmically on that apparatus which

58

forced the wind whistling up through the flames.

As he worked, he spoke; and presently Lester waved Red Hawk into the shop.

He approached close to the fire-handler. A hot, sulphurous damp oppressed his lungs.

"Young feller," said Sam Calkins's thick voice, "it don't mean much to me to have an apprentice hangin' around—white *or* Injun. Mostly, they're only in the way, and the minute that they learn enough to make a weld they go off somewhere and set up for themselves. It ain't funny. It's a sad thing, when you think about the tons of iron that fools spoil every year in the world. If a new man comes to work for me, he's gotta stay till he's a smith, or I don't want him."

"How long would that be?" asked Lester.

Sam Calkins's bulging eyes retracted behind their lids, for an instant. Then he said:

"This here long."

In the grasp of one fist he swayed his hammer in a wide arc, so that it swept up through the air and dropped down as though to batter against his own upraised chin. But at the last moment, with an exertion of power that made his arm and all his vast shoulder tremble, Sam Calkins checked the impetus so that the bright steel face of the hammer-head touched his jaw lightly.

He twisted it back through an arc and laid it back in place against the wall.

"When he can do that he's blacksmith enough to suit me," said Calkins, and his glance traveled over the slender body of Red Hawk.

"He's not a Hercules," said Lester, smiling. "Do you think you'd want to stay here until you could do that trick, Red Hawk?"

Red Hawk lifted the hammer in one hand.

"To do such a thing is medicine, not the strength of a

horse or of a fool," Red Hawk said slowly. He put down the hammer and waved his hand toward the blacksmith. "I shall stay with him till I learn."

Sam Calkins said nothing; he merely grinned until his thick lips were pulled out thin, like rubber.

"Ten dollars a month—and a man's pay after he learns," said Calkins. Then he added with a fierce scowl, "But if he tries to walk out before his time's up, I'm gonna go after him—Injun or white—and have him back to his work. I gotta spend brains to make a blacksmith out of a damn young fool, and I ain't gonna spend brains for nothing."

"This may be hard work," said Lester to Red Hawk. "It may even be harder than you'll want to do. But if you go through with it, you'll be ready for a life among us. Do you want to try it? You hear what Sam Calkins says. If you start, you'll have to finish to his satisfaction."

It seemed to Red Hawk that he stood again in the medicine lodge; that Running Elk, with a blood-dripping hand, had grasped him by the right breast and again asked him if he wished to endure the test that would prove him a man. That was why he cried out with a sudden eagerness that he would attempt this thing.

"All right," said Sam Calkins. "If there's enough wear in you, you'll be the man for me. If there ain't enough wear, I'll throw you out quick enough. You can stay in the shack with me and the old woman. We'll feed you and board you, and you'll get ten dollars a month for pay."

Red Hawk walked back to the door with Lester.

"My brother, you have been very kind to me," he said. "He who honors a stranger honors himself; and now you have given me to a great medicine man who will make me wise. What shall I give you? The gray stallion which carried me from the country of the Cheyennes. He is yours. I am to be a man who lives on the ground for a long time,

60

and the horse is yours."

Red Hawk said no more; and he was astonished at Lester's reaction.

Lester protested, until he saw a darkness of incredulity and anger come into the eyes of Red Hawk. Then he realized that to refuse the present would be an unforgivable insult; so at last he went up the street.

Once, however, he paused, turned, and looked back towards Red Hawk with an anxious eye.

CHAPTER 10

IT was nearly all sledgehammer work. Red Hawk raised blisters the first day, broke them the second, and, after that, worked for a week with bleeding hands. He had never been through anything like it.

Gradually the skin toughened. The muscles of his arms and shoulders and back were drawn to agony from the second day forward, but even these relaxed. For three mornings he had known when he dragged his eyes open that on this day he could no longer stand at the anvil, swinging the heavy sledge while Sam Calkins's light striking hammer tapped remorselessly on, pointing out the places where the ponderous sledge must beat, cursing in thundering tones when the blows which Red Hawk's numb arms delivered fell awry.

But every day Red Hawk managed to get his protesting body from the blankets by telling himself that this was better than being dragged by rawhide tied into his flesh around and around the medicine lodge. And every day there was one moment of grace when Maisry Lester passed by the blacksmith shop, morning or afternoon, and either paused to call out a greeting or else came in and talked for an instant. He hid the bloodstained handle of the hammer from her on these occasions, and kept his hands from view.

For the rest, there was nothing but a dark obscurity of effort, more than he could endure until he sat with Sam Calkins and his wife at meals.

Mrs. Calkins had a nose like a beak, and the eyes of a bird set close in at the roots of it. She was as lean and dark as her husband was gross and fair; and no matter what the talk, her rapid glances counted the mouthfuls which Red Hawk lifted to his lips.

At night Red Hawk always crawled into the icy waters of the creek that ran behind the house, washed himself, and took his trembling body back to the shack and up the ladder to the attic, where he slept on a straw pallet, in a twist of his own buffalo robe. He felt that he was being tried by cold fire, and hammered into a new shape; but he was young enough to accept this as something good for the soul.

It was not altogether the brutality of Sam Calkins that forced his apprentice through these bitter times. There was also a great need, because Sam had undertaken to provide the ponderous ironwork for a number of prairie schooners. That was why the fire burned so big in the forge. If Sam demanded the labor of two men from his apprentice he exacted the toil of four from his own great body.

Then came the day when there arrived, instead of the men who were to pay for his heavy labor, a letter from them cancelling the order. Straightway disaster fell upon Red Hawk.

There was no one else for Sam to curse and abuse except the pack of idlers who were generally gathered all day long about the doors to see the "white Indian" at work. It must have been the devil himself who put into the hands of the blacksmith the sheep-shears, as he strode up and down the shop, grinding his teeth, staring at the heaped masses of the iron-work for which he would not be paid.

Sam Calkins's angrily working fingers made the blades of the shears grind back and forth with a slight twanging sound, which impelled him to look about for something to cut.

A throat would have been more to his taste, but at last he saw the thick, ropy braids of the dark red hair of his apprentice, as that youth worked patiently, drilling holes for rivets through a flat slab of wrought iron. So Sam Calkins, with a gesture and a wink, drew the attention of the idlers to what he was about to do. He stepped up behind his assistant, and, with a double snip of the keen shears, severed the two braids close to the head. Then he leaped back with a shout of derision.

"That'll cool your head for you in this hot weather!" cried Sam.

A whooping chorus of mirth roared into the shop as Red Hawk turned and looked at the fallen braids, putting one hand on the naked nape of his neck. To be without long hair was hardly to be a Cheyenne; one was no more than a squaw in mourning.

It took him two or three seconds to understand what had happened, but when he fully knew the extent of the desecration he snatched out his knife and went at Sam Calkins like a tiger. The flash of the sharp steel made Calkins bolt. There would not have been enough speed in his legs to escape; it was only chance that as Red Hawk hurled the knife Calkins stumbled. That was why the weapon shot past his ear in a long line of light that went out when the blade drove deep into the wall and remained there, humming like a hornet.

63

The sight of it made Calkins bound like a deer through the scattering crowd at the door and into the sunlight, before he recovered himself and turned to face his apprentice.

Red Hawk, as he raced in, shouted out in exultation; for the test had come at last, and in his heart there was no fear of this huge man, but only joy. That cry was still on his lips when a bystander struck a blow for the blacksmith.

The man simply grasped the loaded butt of the black-snake that hung over his neck and caught one of Red Hawk's ankles with the twining lash of it. Red Hawk dived into the dust, and Sam Calkins fell on top of him.

That was all there was to the fight. One hammerhanded stroke rolled darkness over the brain of Red Hawk. He knew nothing of the blows that followed, battering his face and crushing his body, until he was roused from the trance by being soused in the tempering tub of dirty water. Then he was allowed to stand, wavering, while the pain from the many cuts and bruises stung his brain back to life.

Little by little, he was able to know what had happened from the brutal outcry of pleasure that was still being raised by the people at the doors, and from the bawling voice of Sam Calkins as the blacksmith cried:

"There's one lesson for you! And the next time you raise the tip of your little finger, you damn murderin' snake of a fake Injun, I'm gonna twist the neck off of your shoulders! Pick up that there drill—and git back to work!"

There was one cause for joy—the free Cheyennes had not seen him beaten like a dog. Only the eyes of the whites had observed him. Then, as lightning divides a storm, so another interpretation gleamed across the darkness of his mind.

He had fled from shame among the Cheyennes only to find shame among the whites; and therefore, it was clear, he was in the hands of the spirits. They had condemned him to pain which must be endured. They had permitted him to be overwhelmed at the very moment when he had assured himself that no matter how he had feared torture, at least he was not afraid of a fighting man. All the bulk of Sam Calkins had not overawed him; then chance had put him down.

As he thought of these things, and as the certainty of his fate came over him, he lifted his hands to the blinding radiance of the sun that gleamed through a rent in the roof of the shop.

"Listeners above, and my father, the sun," said he, in Cheyenne. "I am your child, and I accept the punishment. Do not be angry with me forever. I make this vow to you: for twelve moons no words shall pass through my throat, neither the white man's speech nor the good Cheyenne. Only I must now warn this man who stands here. When the twelve moons have gone by, if you are pleased with me, give strength to my hands so that they may destroy this man."

He turned with a calm face towards the blacksmith, saying: "The Sky People are angry with me. They have made me a dog to be beaten. For twelve moons I shall continue to be the dog which you kick out of your way. At the end of that time I shall kill you if I can, my father!" His lips were sealed.

That same afternoon Lester came to the blacksmith shop and spoke sternly and rapidly to Sam Calkins. The smith blustered at first, then stood red and silent. Afterwards, Lester came to Red Hawk.

"Come with me, my friend," said the lawyer. "I've heard of what has happened. Come home with me and we'll find a better place for you."

But Red Hawk, looking straight into the eyes of the white man, shook his head.

He would not speak, and at last the force of his silence pressed Richard Lester backwards out of the shop. He went off with a puzzled air, and at that Sam Calkins began to grin. The grin did not last long, however, for when he examined the face of Red Hawk he felt that the callow boy was dead, and that a man stood in his place.

Maisry came the next morning. She did not so much as glance at the blacksmith, but standing in front of Red Hawk, she said to him, anxiously:

"Will you speak to me? Are you silent because you hate us? Do you think we sent you to work here because we wanted to get you off our hands quickly? Red Hawk, we are all very sad about you. Will you speak?"

Her face was full of sympathy.

He looked her straight in the eye. The very roots of his heart were torn with a desire to talk to her, but the oath of silence held him. At last she shrank out of the place as her father had done before her.

CHAPTER 11

AFTER that point, it is necessary to think of the twelve months that passed over the body and soul of Red Hawk as of time dreamed away. His hands were busy enough, and so were his wits, for if he had not studiously employed himself, he would have gone mad.

Even in the night, sometimes the fierceness of his longing for the Cheyennes and the great plains and the happy, free life started him up from his sleep and then he would pacify himself by going down in the middle hours of darkness to work in the shop at the forge. He came to know how to read the mind and heart inside of iron by the way its color changed in heating and cooling, and by the way his hammer sprang upwards from a blow. In a month he had learned more than Sam Calkins had ever been able to teach any apprentice in two years, because the passion of his industry was the passion of his hatred for the whites and his yearning for the red men of the plains.

There was only one flaw in the perfection of that detestation of white men, and that was the feeling he had for the Lesters. Yet when Richard Lester came into the shop regularly once a month, Red Hawk turned to him a face as cold and hard as iron, and kept his vowed silence. It was simply because he felt inside himself a womanish weakness which, if he made a single sign, might burst out as through a broken dam into a confession of loneliness and bitterness of heart.

As for the girl, she came no more, and the thought of her drew on his heart with wonderful power. However, he found a way of seeing her without being seen, for one Sunday when the music began to thunder in the church, he climbed among the branches of a pine tree near the building and looked through the window. There he saw the organist with pumping feet and rapid fingers; there he saw the chorus standing, with the girl among them. Only one face was not deformed by the making of song and that was hers.

Every Sunday, after that, he lay among the branches of the pine trees and listened and looked. So she put out root in his heart, and the thought of her flowered in his mind until sometimes the songs she had sung worked in his throat and her image came between him and the white-hot shining of the iron on the anvil.

He had come to the village a stranger. He grew more strange in it as time went on. Sometimes the keen edge of

67

his vow roused him out of sleep choking with the desire for speech. All he could do was to fill his hands, so he would hurry down to the shop.

When the heavy hammer began to ring in the smithy in the middle of the night, the neighbors would waken suddenly and stare at the blackness about them, with the feeling that a devil possessed the apprentice.

If he was a stranger to the entire village, he was no less a stranger to Sam Calkins and Mrs. Calkins. She in a fury, had refused to sit at table with a tongueless beast, and dumped his rations for the day into a bucket.

"The only way that swine had oughta be fed!" she shrilled at him.

Because he accepted this silently and calmly, it became the custom. He would take the pail with whatever was thrown into it, and sitting cross-legged on the little back porch of the house, eat his food alone.

As for Sam Calkins, he was never at ease when his back was turned to this silent apprentice. He took pleasure in showing an occasional feat of strength before Red Hawk, but if he bent an iron bar with his naked hands or twisted a horseshoe, he found that the eyes of his assistant remained half blank and half vaguely smiling. Nervousness therefore grew in Calkins's mind. He even talked the matter over with his wife.

"Why should I have a damn Injun around to cut my throat some night?"

And she answered, "Ain't he three men for the work he does—at a quarter the cost of one? And ain't you man enough to take care of yourself, you great hulk?"

It was midwinter when there walked into the blacksmith shop a huge man dressed in deerskins, with a knife at his belt and a gun in his hand. He had the flowing hair of the frontiersman, and in his face such savagery as Red Hawk

68

never had seen before—not even in the withered, evil features of Running Elk, the medicine man. But with the cruelty, the set iron of that face, there was combined dignity such as goes with the endurance of pain.

Stepping close to Red Hawk, he paused there, towering above, his glance burning into the eyes of the lad.

"Is this the Cheyenne?" asked the stranger, suddenly.

"He's got a white skin, Mr. Sabin—under the soot," said the blacksmith. "But he's got a damned red Cheyenne heart inside of him!"

"When he grows long hair and puts on paint, I'll find him again!" said Sabin, and strode out of the blacksmith shop.

That was the way in which Red Hawk for the first time encountered the Wind Walker face to face; and as he saw the giant stepping away, he knew that he had been closer to death than ever before in his life.

The house of Marshall Sabin, whom the Cheyennes called Wind Walker, was in the bottom of a small hollow at the edge of the town. Sometimes, in the very early morning, or in the dusk of the day, Red Hawk would go through the trees and to the edge of the hollow and look down at the little shack. That was as far as his feet ever took him, but in his daydreams he often walked down the slope and beat on the door of the house and saw it opened by the giant. As an ordinary youth might have dreamed of becoming a king, so he dreamed of the glory that would come to the slayer of Wind Walker, the great enemy of the Cheyennes. But even in dreams he could hardly enlarge his mind to the thought of facing Wind Walker single-handed.

To the end, Red Hawk was like a scout in a hostile land, and therefore he moved about the village chiefly by night. For one thing, that enabled him to avoid the critical eyes and the loud, yelling voices of the boys. For another, he ran no chance of meeting Maisry or her father, whom he did not wish to hurt with his silence, as he must do, by his vow.

In the shop, on Sundays, he was alone and could work for himself. He spent much time and skill in forging a huge sixteen-inch knife for his own purposes.

For the rest, he amused himself by swinging a fourteen-pound sledge backhand, making it come down towards his chin gently. But at the last moment the impetus of the heavy hammer could not be quite checked, and the apprentice had to duck his head out of the way. His strength had not yet mounted to the point which his master demanded of him, but it was near the mark. He was no longer the sleek creature that had come to Witherell from the plains. Hard labor, for endless hours every day, had changed his muscles to tendons, and his tendons to bone. His limbs were embraced, as it were, by the long, many-fingered hands of strength; and twenty times a day he tested himself by attempting the feat of the hammer.

The spring turned to full summer. The burning days turned the hills brown. The "fair," which this year was very late, filled the streets of Witherell with noise and people. Red Hawk, in the evenings, went through the town, walking slowly past lighted windows and open doors to get a glimpse of the life inside the saloons. He saw trappers who had come in from a distance, their faces sun-browned until they were almost as dark as Indians.

From the two dance-halls he heard music swinging, and laughter and the whispering or the trampling of many crowding feet. And at such moments an ache of loneliness would come over his heart.

But now the time was not long. The twelve moons were completed. Tomorrow, if he chose, he could attempt the feat of the sledge-hammer before the eyes of Sam Calkins, and after that—well, there would be no scoundrel to trip him when he fought with Sam Calkins the second time.

CHAPTER 12

ONE evening, returning from the town, he had come almost to the door of the house when an obscure, sleepy night noise of a bird drifted to him from the nearest tree.

He whirled and crouched to see more clearly. Then he stole through the darkness towards the tree, gasping:

"Brother, is it you?"

A shadow stepped out from behind the tree trunk. "It is I," said the soft voice of Standing Bull.

Under the double darkness of the tree, Red Hawk gripped the two hands of his friend. "Brother!" was all he could say. "Brother, brother! Is it well with you?"

"It is well with me," said Standing Bull. "And it is well with you. Red Hawk is so happy among his people that he forgets the Cheyennes."

"There is no happiness except seeing you again," said Red Hawk. "But why should I speak of myself? I want to know about the Cheyennes. Tell me about my people. Tell me of Spotted Antelope and Bitter Root!"

"Spotted Antelope found twenty buffalo in a gully. One end of it was backed against a bank they could not climb. The other end he blocked with fire. He killed them all. His tepee is filled with robes and meat, and there is pemmican for years in their lodge. The weak and the sick are fed by your father's hand; your mother keeps a strong fire

71

burning all day long, and the meat pot is always full for the hungry."

"I am glad!" said Red Hawk.

"They send messages to you, brother," said the Cheyenne. "Return to them. Their spirits are empty. The days go by like swift, muddy waters. They wait in the lodge for you."

"And Lazy Wolf? Is he fortunate?" asked Red Hawk, after a silence.

Standing Bull laughed a little, saying, "He has a new lodge. He has more horses. He has a strong wagon which carries his lodge and all that he possesses. The Blue Bird drives the horses, and laughs."

"And all the tribe?" asked Red Hawk.

"They are sad, a little," said Standing Bull. "Wind Walker comes behind us as the shadow comes behind a cloud. He has killed four more of our young men."

"And the braves? And Dull Hatchet?" cried Red Hawk, anxiously.

"They have ridden by day and night. The horses are lean. A man can put his fist in the hollow between the hip bone and the small ribs. But still they cannot take Wind Walker. He blows away from them. If they come too close, his rifle kills the best man in the hunt, and then he rides on again."

Red Hawk groaned. "And now, for yourself?" he demanded.

"I saw a Pawnee in a hollow draw, by a water hole," said Standing Bull. "He was a Pawnee wolf. I called, and as he turned he died. I took his scalp. I saw two Blackfeet on the head of a mountain. As they rode down the mountainside they came into an alley among the tall trees, and there they died. On one of them I counted the grand coup."

"Ah, friend!" cried Red Hawk enthusiastically, "there

72

is no other like you in the tribe. Every year you are richer in coups; you are greater in honor! But what were you doing so near the setting sun? Why were you in the land of the Blackfeet, among the mountains? Were you taken there by some great vow?"

"The White Horse," said the Cheyenne, with a sigh. "I have followed him for nine months. Five horses died under me—and he is still free!"

Red Hawk's mind saw again the swift-driven herd of horses, like a flying lance, with the white stallion as the gleaming point of the spear. "I have dreamed of him, also," he said.

"Except in a dream, no man will ride him," said the Cheyenne. "Brother, I drove him down a narrow gorge, and my heart was dying with joy because at the end of the gorge the ground fell away at a waterfall. He turned to charge back past me, but the swinging of my rawhide rope turned him again. He went galloping swiftly, and when he came to the edge of the waterfall he was neighing; he was calling death; he was leaping through the empty air into freedom.

"I rode to the edge of the falls and looked down. I saw the great white horse spinning in the current below. He fought to climb the bank. The slippery mud threw him back. The water tore at him. I began to shout and sing for him. I offered a sacrifice of a good buffalo robe if the underwater people would spare him; and a moment later he was galloping away across the grass of the lower valley.

"I saw that he was not for me, and I came back to my people. Except for that long hunt, I should have come to find you long before this. Now talk of yourself. Who are your friends?"

"There are none," said Red Hawk. "One man befriended me. I paid him with a gift of the gray horse. Then in a few days I went to work as white men do, in the shop of the blacksmith. He clipped off my hair and made me like a woman who mourns. I threw a knife and missed him. I went to fight him, and another man tripped me. I was beaten.

"I vowed to the spirits that I would live twelve moons in suffering, so that they would no longer be angry with me. I have been as silent as a beast, but perhaps the listeners above and underground are pleased with me. Now the twelve moons of my vow have passed. If my prayer has been heard, tomorrow I shall kill the man who calls himself my master. Then I shall be free."

To this crowded recital, Standing Bull listened without a word, keeping silence for a long time after. At last he simply said, "And then?"

"Then, if I go free, I shall not return to the Cheyennes until I have done some great deed."

"What deed, brother?"

"Something which will make me appear as a man among the Cheyennes. When I can think what to do, I shall make a vow."

"Great vows make weary hearts!" said Standing Bull. "But you fight a man tomorrow. Shall I help you to kill him? The honor and the first coup shall be yours, but I shall help!"

"No," said Red Hawk. "Because I have marked him every day since the first day. Tomorrow I shall kill him or he will kill me. As for you, go over the hills. Ride up the length of Witherell Creek until you come to the fallen house and the white stone on the ground. Wait for me there for three days. If I have not come, I am dead or worse than dead; therefore go away and forget me."

He waited a long time before he had the answer. He waited so long that he asked, "How did you find me?"

74

"I hunted the white camp with my eyes for three days before I found your place," said Standing Bull. "Farewell, brother."

The eyes of Red Hawk had grown dim and the beat of his pulse filled his ears, so that he neither heard nor saw the going of his friend; he merely knew that he was alone. Afterwards, he went to the bank of the creek, and for a long time watched the stars appear and disappear in the still water near the bank.

He could not go back into Sam Calkins's house because already he was killing that man in his mind. Therefore he sat down with his back to a tree, his face towards the east, and went to sleep with his chin on his breast.

CHAPTER 13

In the dawn, a dog came out from the village and barked at Red Hawk. He stood up and lifted his arms towards the growing fire in the east. Minutes went slowly by him.

His heart was comforted when he went to the blacksmith shop. There he sat cross-legged on the floor until Sam Calkins came out, bellowing:

"You been gadding, have you? Well, it's too damn late for any breakfast now. And what the hell you mean by not havin' the fire goin' at this time of day?"

Red Hawk got to his knees, laid his hands palm down on the ground, prayed for ten silent seconds, and rose to his feet. He went to the row of hammers that leaned against the wall, and picked out the fourteen-pound sledge. This he swayed ever so lightly through the air until, from the

75

top of its rise, it came wavering slowly down, checked by all the rigid power in his arm. It touched his chin, gently. Then he threw it aside.

"By the Great Horn Spoon!" shouted Sam Calkins. "It ain't possible! It ain't—"

Red Hawk went up to him. "Now," said Red Hawk, "I have completed my vow to remain silent, and I must kill you. Are you ready?"

"Ready? *Hai*, you drunk fool of a stinkin' Injun!" shouted Sam Calkins, and he smote upwards with all his might, rising on his toes to fling his weight into the blow.

By the clearness with which he saw that massive fist coming, and by the cold calmness in his eyes and heart, Red Hawk knew that the spirits had heard his prayer. He stepped aside to let the danger jump past his face, then he caught Sam Calkins with the crook of his arm around the throat.

When they went down, the bulk of Calkins fell on Red Hawk and knocked the wind out of his body, but the White Indian only locked his stranglehold the tighter. Calkins's terrible hands gripped at him, at the lean, iron bar of his forearm, sunk in the bulging throat. But presently the hands made no further efforts, except to claw vaguely at the air; and at last they fell limply down.

"He is mine!" said Red Hawk to his heart, "and he is soon dead. But I have lived in his lodge; I have eaten his food; he has taught me his medicine!"

He slid from beneath the man's limp weight, and sat on the edge of the tempering tub, looking down at the blacksmith's black, swollen face. He began to dip his hand into the black water of the tub and throw it over the face and body of Sam Calkins, thoughtfully, for he was wondering why he could not kill the man. Also, he wondered whether or no the fulfilling of his vow did not demand the killing.

But by the peace in his heart, he judged that all was well.

Sam Calkins began to breathe audibly, dragging in his breath with a rattling noise. His face turned from dark purple to blue.

The voice of Mrs. Calkins said, suddenly, "Why didn't you kill the great beast, Red Hawk? Nobody would 'a' missed him."

He saw, then, that she was standing just inside the back door, and by some leaping of the mind he knew that she had been there from the first moment of the fight.

"You wanta be paid off?" she said. "Well, I'll fetch you the money. It's a hundred and twenty dollars, because nary a penny has that fat swine paid you. But *I'll* pay."

When she came back from the house, she put twelve golden eagles into Red Hawk's hand.

Her husband remained propped in a half-sitting posture, no longer rattling in his throat, but groaning with every breath he drew. His wife went to him and prodded him in the ribs with the toe of her boot.

"Get up, pig!" she said. "Go and drool your blood over your work, and not on the ground. I'm glad to see the color of that blood in you. If ever you lift hand at *me* again, I'll take a knife and see the same color, too. Get up, bully—beast—lounging, cowardly loafer!"

Red Hawk was amazed to see the hulk of the man rise, stagger, and go blindly towards the forge. It sickened Red Hawk to see him, so he went hastily out into the sun of the early morning. He could join Standing Bull now! But he must not come like a ragged beggar.

He went to a store and bought a deerskin suit, new moccasins, a good rifle, plenty of ammunition, and an Indian saddle with the rawhide stretched so tightly over the crossed sticks of the pommel and cantle that the skin was semi-translucent.

After that there still remained a great deal of money, so he went to the horse dealer at the end of the village and hunted through the herd in the great corral until he found what he wanted, a shaggy pony with a ewe neck, a roached back, and an eye of red fire. What Red Hawk wanted and bought, however, were not these traits; they were the four strong legs and the depth of the barrel, which indicated endurance. No white man in the world—not even a trapper from the plains—would have selected such a savage little beast; but Red Hawk knew the qualities which enable a horse to endure winter and summer and hard riding.

He saddled the horse, rode the kinks out of it in a brisk ten minutes of pitching, and took it out of the village and up the creek. There he tethered it in some tall brush.

There were two gifts of the white man that he had learned to appreciate during his residence in the town. One was a comb with smooth teeth, and the other was soap. Now he stripped to his skin, and began to scrub. There was grime and grease and soot, here and there—the signs of the blacksmith shop—but he was not scrubbing this away. He was washing himself clean of all his days among the whites, of all the humiliation, the shame, the sorrow and the foulness that comes out of a brooding mind.

When he ended, he moved out of the flow of the current and stepping into the slack, still waters near the shore, he saw his image. The brown of the prairie years had gone from his body, and he was startled by the white flash of his skin as the water reflected it. He leaned over to study details.

The Indian life, on foot or horseback, gives strength to the legs; the laboring white man clothes his arms and shoulders with muscles. And now Red Hawk saw that a thousand interlacing fingers embraced his shoulders and ribs and ran with long taperings down his arms. The swaying of the fourteen-pound sledge had put hard fists in the pit of his belly. He felt a sudden joy, as though he were looking at another man, a champion, say, ready to ride into battle on behalf of the Cheyennes.

His face was much older, too. Pain had darkened his forehead and shadowed his eyes and stiffened his upper lip. He looked like an older and a wiser brother of that Red Hawk who had laughed and played among the Cheyennes.

As if to wash that unhappy picture of himself from his mind, he dived suddenly into the creek, with nothing on his body except that sacred amulet, that medicine stone, the green beetle which hung from the leather thong about his neck.

When he came out of the cold depths, he regarded the sun. It would soon turn him bronze again. A few weeks of the old life and he would be no longer white as a fungus on the under side of a fallen tree; white as the belly of a frog that lives in the slime of a pool. Darkness bleaches all things, and it seemed to Red Hawk that all his days among the whites had been the darkness of eye and spirit.

The sun now warmed him, and the twisting currents had washed his soul clean of the evil which had been around him. All Indian—let him be all Indian! Let all his thoughts be Indian thoughts, and let his body once more assume the dark, brown-red stain which was the fitting color for humanity!

He dressed carefully, and rejoiced most of all in the feel of the good strong moccasins that embraced his feet. He combed out his hair, last of all, and he was amazed to see how well it had grown, during this year. It was almost as though the filthy shears of the blacksmith never had despoiled his head.

Having finished, he filled his pipe with more than the mere ceremonial gestures, and smoked the pipe out.

He had finished and disjointed the stem from the clay when he heard voices coming up the side of the creek—the deep speech of men, and the voice of a girl.

He drew back into the brush, and saw Maisry Lester come into the cove. She walked between the two Bailey brothers. As he crouched lower, he found himself fingering the great sixteen-inch knife which he had made for his special use. He was glad of the savage impulse, for it gave him the last proof that the call of blood had no power over him. Or was it perhaps a strange reaction because he saw the girl with the two men? This thought disturbed him.

"Here's a good place," said Jeremy Bailey. "We can talk it out here, Joe."

"Aye. This ought to do," said Joe Bailey, and he fixed a scowl on his brother.

They had the look of men about to fight, thought Red Hawk, and in that case it would be a fight worth seeing. For they were both of a bigness, with an equal loftiness, and the same weight of shoulders. Being twins, they also had the same flaxen hair and blue eyes. Even their voices had a kindred quality. But Jeremy had the brains of the pair. It was he who had built up the big Bailey trading post by his ventures, though the stamp which distinguished him from his brother was mainly a scar on his forehead, like a slanting stroke of red paint.

"Why should we stop here?" said the girl. "If there's anything to talk about—especially—we can do that as we walk along."

"We've got to face each other and an important idea," said Jeremy.

"What idea?" asked Maisry.

"He's right," said Joe Bailey. "The only other thing that he's ever had the good taste to agree with me about is you,

Maisry. That's why we've managed to get you out here alone."

She looked from one to the other. Red Hawk drew closer in the brush.

"We've been wrangling," explained Jeremy. "And it's about you. Probably you don't care a rap about either of us. But if you're interested in either Joe or me, tell us which one, so that the other fellow can cancel himself out. I ought to find a prettier way of saying all this, but I'm not romantic. I'm a business man, Maisry."

"You mean—" she said, "that really—?" She made a gesture towards them, and then touched her breast lightly. "You really mean that you both think— Why, I can't say— I've known you a long time, Jeremy and Joe. You know I respect you both—and admire you both, too."

"Think a bit, Maisry," said Jeremy. "This is the time to cancel out one of us. It's not committing yourself to the other fellow."

"Don't be so swift and bitter about it, Jeremy," cautioned his brother. "Confound it, this isn't bargaining for buffalo hides! But do you think you care especially for either of us, Maisry?"

"I'm flattered—and a bit giddy," said the girl. She seemed to be thinking the thing out carefully, bit by bit, and she kept looking them in the eye. "But, oh, it's a thousand miles from the real thing, you know!"

"What's the real thing? Love?" asked Jeremy. "Well, outside of books, what does it all amount to?"

She smiled, at that. She said, "Well, it's a jump of the heart and a stopping of the breath, at least."

"Hold on!" said Joe. "Did any other man ever make your heart jump, ever stop your breath?"

She hesitated.

81

"You don't have to answer," said Joe. "But I'd like to know."

"I'll answer," she said. "Yes there was one man."

"And he still does?"

"No, no!" she cried.

The two brothers exchanged glances.

"There's no use pushing ahead," said Joe. With divining eyes he kept probing at her. "But if you don't mind, you're not seeing the last of us. However, you might tell us something that would drop both of us or one of us out of the list at once. What sort of a man would you like to think of?"

"I don't know," she answered. "The sort of a man that any woman would admire, I suppose."

"What sort of a man would that be?"

"Why—that's hard to say. I suppose"—and here she threw back her head suddenly—"oh, I suppose the sort of a man who could catch the White Horse and bring him in!"

"*Hai!*" cried Jeremy Bailey. "Who would have thought that?"

But Red Hawk, as he heard the White Horse mentioned, had involuntarily started up. He felt the startled eyes of the girl on his face, and he dropped out of sight again, instantly. Then he waited for her to cry out to the others.

But no outcry came from her.

"Women are like that, I suppose," chuckled Joe Bailey. "Well, had we better start back?"

"I'm going to stay here alone for a while," said the girl. "If you don't mind, I'd rather be here alone."

The Baileys went off. Only Jeremy paused for an instant beside Maisry. His color had changed so that the red scar was painted on his face much more brightly than before.

"We'll come to see you *and* your father tomorrow," he said.

Presently Red Hawk came out of the brush.

The girl began to back away from him with small steps. She had the look of one who wants to run away, but who knows that flight is useless.

"Why are you afraid?" asked Red Hawk.

"If they had found you, there—!" said she. "That was why I was afraid. Did you follow us?"

That suggestion made him very angry. "A Cheyenne," he told her, "does not follow a woman. If he wants her, he goes to her father's lodge and ties a present of horses near the entrance. Or he brings buffalo robes or guns. He does not go like a hunting cat, stealthily, as the white men do!"

"But *you* are not Cheyenne," she answered.

"My skin is white, but my heart is red," said he.

He pointed to the running water. The shimmering reflection of it kept a pale tremor of light in the foliage and over the face and figure of the girl.

"But now I have washed away a year among the whites," said he. "That year has flown away down the stream and left me a pure Cheyenne. Now I may go back to my people."

"But if you go," she told him, "do you mean that you are leaving the white men forever? Are you going to live in tents, and to shiver in winter and starve when the buffalo cannot be found? Are you going out to paint yourself blue and red, and to take scalps and—and raise—half-breed children?"

There seemed to be sorrow as well as disgust in her. That was why he made no answer at first. Then he said:

"You white people like to have four walls around you. You measure out your days into little hours that keep hurrying away from you. The only thing that can open your eyes is gold! Well, I don't like your way of living. I could show you a better way, because there is plenty of Indian in you."

"In me?" she cried.

"You want the White Horse. That is the sort of a wish that would come to a Cheyenne maiden—a girl who is the daughter of a great chief. That is what she might wish, looking away from the herds of her father; looking at the edge of the sky; and wishing for the White Horse. That was why my heart opened when I first saw you."

He came up close to her. The closer he came, the wider stretched her eyes.

"Are you afraid of me?" asked Red Hawk.

"No," she answered.

"You are afraid," he contradicted. "But that is foolish. You could make me unhappy. You are all that I leave behind me among the whites. When I stood in the running water—you see?—it carried away from me all of the year I have lived among white men. It carried the noise of the blacksmith shop out of my ears, but it left your voice in them. I have been in the tree outside the church, even in winter, and I have heard you singing. So why should you be afraid of me now?"

"I am not afraid," said the girl. She looked down at the river and joined her hands together.

"Ha!" cried Red Hawk, softly. "When I stand close to you, a happiness comes into me. I drink up happiness like the dry prairies when the first good rain comes in the autumn. It makes me strong. I am going away—but I shall return!

"You are in the midst of the time when the looks of a woman comes into the eyes of a girl and the young men watch her as she walks. The woman comes into the throat of a girl, and the young men are starved with hope. But be patient. I am going away as far as the edge of the world, but perhaps I shall bring something back to you. Farewell!"

CHAPTER 14

HE left Maisry and got swiftly to his mustang. But he had one other thing to do before he got away from Witherell.

He went to the house of the lawyer, Richard Lester, whom he found pacing up and down the path in front of his house with hands clasped behind his back.

Red Hawk had dismounted, tethered the mustang and entered the yard before Lester was aware of him. For a moment there was no recognition in Lester's face. Then he came suddenly to himself and took the hand of the youth, saying:

"I've heard that Sam Calkins has lost an apprentice and learned the taste of his own blood. It may make a better man of him. But why are you dressed like this, Red Hawk? As if you were becoming an Indian again!"

"I leave the whites and return to my own people," said Red Hawk simply.

"Your own people! Why, my friend, you have a whiter skin than most of us! Why do you talk of leaving? To join the traders, perhaps? To use your Indian knowledge in order to make your fortune? Surely not to return to the Cheyennes!"

"Why should I try to make a fortune?" asked Red Hawk.

"Why? Well, because money can buy any comfort. It builds homes, feeds children, and—"

He paused to gather more ideas, and Red Hawk answered, "The best lodge is that which a man's squaw makes for him; the best meat is that which a man shoots and his woman cooks. Money cannot buy a north wind in summer or a south wind in winter . . ."

The lofty brow of the lawyer gathered into wrinkles of pain and of thought.

Then Red Hawk took his hand again, continuing, "Father, farewell. I have made a great vow. Now I am going to hunt it as a hawk hunts a bird in the sky; but if I live, I shall return to look into your face again."

"If you must go," said Richard Lester, "speak to my wife and to Maisry. She has been unhappy about you all this year. Also, take the gray horse; it will be of greater use to you than that shaggy pony."

"No," said Red Hawk. "Men say that a gift is always sad when it returns to the giver. And as for your wife and daughter, when I speak to the master of the lodge, I speak to every one in it. Farewell!"

That was how he left Richard Lester and rode out of the town of Witherell.

At the entrance to the pass through the hills he paused for a moment on the high ground to look back at the roofs of the white lodges. It seemed to Red Hawk that he was looking back upon a prison, or a grimy hand which was closed around a single bright thing. Then he pointed the head of the fiery-eyed pony into the pass and put it to a steady trot.

When he reached the place of the fallen sod house, the heat of the day had gone; the color of the evening had burned up in tall flames and sunk towards the horizon in smoke which was still faintly luminous in the sky and on the face of Witherell Creek. From the edge of the high bank of the stream he called loudly.

That call was answered at once. Horse and man came scrambling up from the gorge, and the voice of Standing Bull shouted joyously to him:

"You have counted coup! Tell me that it is so!" said Standing Bull.

"His throat was in the hollow of my arm. I could feel him dying," said Red Hawk, "but then I remembered that I had eaten his food, and so I let him live. Tell me one thing. Have you sat by the white stone that has the writing on it?"

"I have," said the Cheyenne.

"Did the voice come up to you out of the ground?" asked Red Hawk.

"I listened very hard," said Standing Bull, "but all that I could hear was the wind whistling through the hair of my head. My medicine was not good enough to make the voice speak to me."

"I shall go to the stone and sit by it," said Red Hawk.

He sat by the white stone, his hand feeling the heat of the day run out of it and the cold of the night enter it. He closed his eyes, while memory began in him again, like the work of magic. He stood up with a gasping cry.

"I have seen her face, brother! I heard her voice say the word again. The bowstring draws tight in my heart and trembles!"

"Look at the ground and look at the stars," said Standing Bull. "When the ghosts speak, their voices should be heeded. What does the word mean?"

"You may laugh, Standing Bull," said Red Hawk. "The word she speaks is the word which among the whites means the red that covers old iron when it begins to rot away. That is what 'Rusty' means. Brother, I am about to make a great vow."

Kindling a fire no larger than the palm of his hand, Red

87

Hawk sprinkled into it some sweet grass which his friend gave to him; and as the fragrant smoke rose he bathed himself with it. Then he offered four handfuls of it to the corners of the sky, to the earth, to the Listeners Above. After that, he lifted his hands until he could see stars trembling and shining at the tips of his fingers, as he said:

"All you Listeners above and under-ground, this is the vow of Red Hawk—that he will sacrifice to you, now, the thing which is most useful to him. He will sacrifice it to you and to the dead squaw of Wind Walker, whose ghost is my friend. Look well at Red Hawk, because if from this moment you ever see his feet pointed away from the trail, he asks you to strike him with sickness or with fire. Or if ever he turns his face until he has put his hand on the mane of the White Horse."

A faint cry came from Standing Bull, but Red Hawk maintained his attitude for a long time, until the stars began to swim before his eyes.

As his hands fell to his sides, he said, "Tell me, Standing Bull. What is the most precious thing that I have with me, if I am to hunt the White Horse? Is it my gun?"

"No, it is the horse you now have. Oh, my brother, the wise men and the strong men of four great nations—and the white men, also—have hunted the White Horse! He is a medicine horse! He is a ghost! How shall you put your hand on his mane?"

"Hush!" commanded Red Hawk. "Speak no words that come between me and my vow. This is a very hard thing—to sacrifice my horse and go on foot after one that runs like the wind. But after all, it is not by the speed of my horse but by the pain of my body and soul that I shall win the indulgence of the Listeners."

He led the horse, saddled as it was, to the white stone, now but a vague, starlit, blur against the shadow of the ground. The pony he held by the under-jaw, drew the bright length of his knife, and offered its point to the ground and to the sky. Then he drove it deep into the animal's body behind the shoulder. The horse fell.

Red Hawk took up his rifle, a weight of ammunition, and faced the west.

"Rest here till the morning," said Standing Bull, "or else let me make one march with you."

"I must go by myself. When you come to my father's lodge, tell him that when he sees me again I shall be riding the White Horse—unless it has died. But living or dead, I shall either touch the stallion or wander forever."

Briefly, he took the hand of the brave, and then he marched toward the west with a long stride. When he had gone a distance, he heard behind him, faintly, the Cheyenne chant for the dead; and he knew that Standing Bull was singing the lament.

CHAPTER 15

MANY people have heard of the hunting of the White Horse. The two names come ding-dong into the memory, like sound and echo: Red Hawk and the White Horse! It is generally known, also, that the hunt ran from the Canadian River on the south, to the Milk River on the north; up the Yellowstone and the Powder Rivers, and up the forks of the Platte, both North and South. It is also known that the drama was concluded among the Blue Water Mountains.

One thing is true: that all during the first autumn of his hunt, as he drifted vaguely, guided by reports that he picked up from a Cheyenne scouting party and from a white trapper, Red Hawk never had a horse or any other means of transportation. He had walked his clothes to rags when he came into the country of the Blackfeet, in the high mountains; and one day he saw before him the figure of a mighty old buffalo, one of those outcasts from the herds. A gray mist was rolling in the mountain pass, and all was so dim that Red Hawk thought the monster bull was simply turned pale by the fog.

But when his rifle exploded and the bull had fallen, he went up and found that his hand was touching "medicine." For it was a white buffalo, the greatest single treasure that could come into the life of an Indian. Had he had a horse, he would have taken off the priceless hide and cured it as well as he could, then taken it back to the Cheyenne. For that pelt alone would have made him welcome and set him on a pedestal above the other braves. But since he was on foot, he remembered his vow. He merely took off the hide, rolled it up, and went on till he found the smoke of a big Blackfoot camp.

Ordinarily, he would have dodged Blackfeet, because they had as great a passion as any tribe to harvest Cheyenne "hair." However, no matter what enemies they might be, they were a red nation. If they did not use the pelt, it would go to waste.

He walked straight into the camp and told his errand. Fifty or more warriors went pelting out on horseback to find the hide of which he spoke. A full fifty others gathered around the "white Cheyenne" and stared at this man who had made the "Vow of the White Horse."

Many of the whites called any one a fool who would waste his life for the sake of touching a wild horse with his hand; but the Indians could only regard such a man as a hero.

Red Hawk never forgot the great council lodge in which he sat, the three greatest of the Blackfeet medicine men opposite him, and the famous chiefs and warriors on either hand. He was from an enemy tribe, to be sure, but he was "medicine," since no one could commit himself to such a vow as his without becoming to some extent sacred. While they waited, they treated him with much respect; but the whole camp went mad with enthusiasm when the braves who had been sent out returned in triumph, carrying the pelt. It was not strictly white, of course, but the hairs were tipped with silver, so that it made a good approach to the required color.

There was a tremendous commotion. Every woman who touched that hide with a scraper, in the fleshing of it, was thereby half sanctified; it was as good as a big sacrifice in the way of ensuring the birth of children, for instance, or in warding off disease. So all the women in that camp were avid to have a share in the preparation of the robe.

That first night a heavy snow had fallen; and it was still falling as the Blackfeet hewed down big pine trees and built a camp fire whose flames licked the rolling clouds that wandered through the sky. In the light of that blaze they set up the buffalo, with head and hoofs and tail and hide intact.

The medicine men came out and went through their most earth-shaking ceremonies; even the children were yelling with excitement because the arrival of a white buffalo robe was enough to bring good luck to the camp for years and years.

Red Hawk was permitting himself this pause in the hunt for the White Horse partly because he had completely lost the trail, and partly because he was so exhausted by between four and five thousand miles of steady marching that a rest could not be considered unwise. As he sat there in the lodge of the head chief of the Blackfeet, Red Hawk assured himself that all his actions had been under the guidance of Sweet Medicine, the invisible spirit of the Sacred Valley.

If he had failed at the Blood Sacrifice, if he had been a slave for a year and more among the whites, these things were all ordained. Sometimes men are purified by sacrifice; sometimes they are purified by pain and humiliation. It was the latter course that had been chosen for him, and the fall of the white buffalo to his hand was simply the first promise of the spirits that they were pleased with his ways. From that moment he became a convinced fatalist, and he felt that he was in the hands of the gods.

He was with the Blackfeet for a fortnight, putting some flesh on his gaunt ribs, and then word was brought in by a scout that the White Horse had been seen to the south. A troop of picked warriors went out with Red Hawk. For his own use, he had the five finest ponies that could be found in the camp, and the entire population turned out to give him a sendoff.

With a dozen chosen men, he rode south; and two days later he saw, for the second time in his life, the White Horse.

They had ridden through a gully, and as they came out on a level plateau they saw the wild herd scattered, pawing through the snow to get at the grass beneath. Red Hawk knew the clarion call of the stallion. Then he saw the great horse marshal his host till they had been gathered into a dark troop; and once more he saw them fly like a lance, with a shining point.

He, and the Blackfeet with him, rode in pursuit till the horses were staggering under them, but they could not gain on a single one of the fugitives.

The White Horse went south as straight, and almost as

fast, as a migrating wild duck. Red Hawk followed him, hardly pausing to sleep or to eat. In three days half his Blackfeet companions were left behind him. In a week, the hardiest warrior of the lot had fallen hopelessly to the rear, without a farewell.

But Red Hawk still had three horses which were in fair condition, and he clung to the trail. He crossed mountains, deserts, wild plateaus. The exhausted mares and colts of the herd of the White Horse fell back and beside him, by this time mere straggling skeletons. One of his own horses broke its leg in a hole. Another fell down and could not rise. The third, one day, stopped trotting, stopped walking, stood with hanging head. Thereupon he dismounted and went on foot, with only the great White Horse before him.

He followed the stallion out from the mountains and into the sweep of the plains; and still the White Horse was sleek with undiminished strength. Red Hawk kept himself running, but two days later the stallion vanished out of his ken.

It was in midsummer, as he followed a rumor from a trapper towards the north, and as he lay one day exhausted and sleeping, in the red of the evening, that he was roused by a rustling in the dryness of the grass beside him. He opened his eyes to see the russet gold of the sunset light dripping like thin blood over the faces of Indians who had stolen up while he slept. By the headgear he knew that they were Dakotas, those most relentless enemies of the Cheyennes.

"It is the white Cheyenne," said one of the crew, almost reverently. "It is Red Hawk, who follows the Horse. Brother, you are safe among us. Your medicine is strong, and we are your friends!"

The Sioux who had spoken was Rising Bull, and he had

ennobled himself by his treatment of an enemy brave. He could have hung in his lodge the scalp of a famous man, but instead, he honored the stranger. There were not many spare horses in the herd which the young braves drove along the trail of the warriors, but Rising Bull gave two to the white Cheyenne, as well as two pairs of strong moccasins, a new rifle in exchange for the old one, and two pairs of leggings, well made and strong. He filled a bag with parched corn, another with dried meat, and gave to Red Hawk the latest news of the White Horse to come across the plains.

The stallion had raised the herd of Murray Quale, the half-breed squaw man, hunter, and man-killer, and the whole herd had been swept away. Murray Quale was now following the White Horse not to capture but to kill it.

That was the word that sent Red Hawk riding hard into the northwest. It was hardly strange that, since they both followed one trail, he met the half-breed on the way. From a summit among the foothills of the Rockies he had seen the dark, spreading herd in a valley below. He had seen it gather, as he descended the slope, and form again into the familiar flying wedge with the shining lance-point leading the way.

The next day, as he followed the plain trail of the herd, he came on a long-haired frontiersman who balanced a leather-cased rifle across the pommel of his saddle. He rode on a strong mule, with two Indian ponies led behind. This stranger threw the case of his rifle when he heard behind him the hoofs of Red Hawk's horses, and turned a broad face with malignant, scarred features.

Something about the squat, powerful body and the readiness with which the muzzle of the rifle was pointed toward him, told Red Hawk that this was his quarry, though he had received no detailed description of Murray Quale's

94

appearance. It was no more difficult for Murray Quale to spot the "white Indian" with red hair, and he pointed his rifle more directly at the breast of Red Hawk as he yelled:

"Hey, you! Ain't you Red Hawk? Back up that pony and tell me if you ain't Red Hawk!"

Red Hawk drew up the pony slowly. He knew that he had come unwarily upon this man-killer; for now he could not possibly unlimber his own holstered rifle, and since he had no revolver or pistol, he had no weapon except the long knife which he had forged for himself in the shop at Witherell. And what would that be, compared with the straight-driven bullets from the muzzle of Quale's rifle?

"Are you the man called Murray Quale?" he asked, allowing his pony to idle a step or two nearer to the half-breed.

"Keep that hoss in its tracks!" said Quale, sharply. "Maybe you know my name, but *I* know every sneakin' Cheyenne trick in the calendar. You're that fool of a white man who trails the White Horse around, ain't you?"

"I'm following the White Horse."

"If it wasn't for you drivin' him, he'd keep out half the hell that he raises for folks. You know what that herd is that he's got with now? You know who they belong to? To me! And I'm the man that's seen the old mares break down and the colts drop dead, tryin' to foller that white devil. If you got a claim on the White Horse, why don't you keep him up in your corral?"

He began to roll his head from side to side, gathering his wrath to a storm and letting himself blow with it.

"I've never had the White Horse," said Red Hawk. "I've only followed him."

"Like a coyote follows a wolf, like a wolf follows the buffalo—just to enjoy the hell that the White Horse raises!" shouted Murray Quale. "What excuse for livin' is there for a fool like you? What room is there on earth for you? That's what I wanta know!"

He was thrusting his head forward, and narrowing his eyes as though already he was squinting through the sights at his target. Never since Red Hawk had stood in the medicine lodge of the Cheyennes, with the blood-dripping hand of Running Elk grasping his breast, had he felt such terror as was in him now.

But the other experience had been the fear of an unending agony and the dread of shaming himself before many eyes. This was different, for death would enter and leave him on the wing, he knew; it would take his soul with a touch, and his scalp would join the two that now dangled from the bridle reins of the half-breed before him. And what more inducement would this scar-faced beast need for a murder than the desire to take such a scalp as that of Red Hawk, now that the hair had regrown long and heavy?

With his eye, Red Hawk measured the distance between himself and the half-breed; in the nerves of his right hand and arm, he was already drawing and hurling the long knife. He said:

"What have I done to make you angry, Murray Quale? I have never seen you before—so how can I have harmed you?"

"You dirty rat of a Cheyenne!" yelled Murray Quale. "Am I a half-wit? Don't I know that you aim to stop me from puttin' into the White Horse a bullet that'll finish his thieving? What difference does it make to you that he's robbed me of my horse herd? None. You're glad, is what you are. And the first chance you got, you'd sneak on me in the middle of the night and wake me up with a cut throat. There ain't nothing but Cheyenne murder in you, and that's why I'm gonna let a streak of hell right through the middle of you, you—"

It had seemed to Red Hawk that he could delay until he saw the butt of the rifle raised to the hollow of Murray Quale's shoulder, but he was wrong. For warning, he had only the stiff, spreading grin on the half-breed's face as he pulled the trigger, the long rifle still held under his arm.

It was no chance shot, however. For as the Cheyenne marked that stretching leer on the face of the other, and jerked suddenly at his pony, Red Hawk's horse suddenly threw his head up and back, and the ounce of lead struck into bone and brain with a sound like that of an ax cleaving home in a great, soft log. Red Hawk had already brought out the heavy length of his knife; and now he threw it with an overhand motion. The horse crumpled under him; and the next instant he was flung heavily on his side, the loose bulk of the dead horse pinning him by the right leg.

He knew, for an instant, that he was lost; that Murray Quale could kill him easily with whatever torments he chose. Then he began to struggle, planting his left heel against the saddle and thrusting with all his might. He seemed to be stripping his flesh from the bone, and the leg moved hardly an inch. But when he lifted head and shoulders, frantic with curiosity, he saw Murray Quale spilling out of the saddle with a singular looseness, so that when his feet struck the ground his knees sagged and his whole body gave.

With one hand clinging to the stirrup leather, the half-breed turned. His face was like that of one helpless with alcohol; the mouth hung open, the eyes were as dull as leaded glass, and in his side the great knife was buried almost to the hilt. One hand held a skinning knife; the other hand stretched out before him like a man who fumbles for his way through the dark. The skinning knife rose in the swift hand of the half-breed; the flash of the steel went down past Red Hawk's eyes, and the knife stood quivering in the ground.

Red Hawk snatched it out, bewildered, and raised it to strike before he saw that there was no need. For Quale was falling, his body and bones turning to pulp, as it seemed. His knees struck the ground; he buckled into a heap so that his long hair flowed forward from the back of his head.

CHAPTER 16

When Red Hawk was free to rise, before he so much as drew his knife from the body of the dead man, he filled a pipe and smoked it in honor of the spirit, Sweet Medicine. The cold of the wind washed over him like running water, but he forgot comfort while he considered that this—knife against rifle—had been a grand coup; such a thing as gives honor to a brave all his life long, and hushes the young men with wonder and envy when the coup is counted.

Then he stood up, put away his pipe, drew the heavy knife from the body of Murray Quale, and looked critically at the point and the edges. Perhaps his heart was colder than the hearts of other men, or perhaps in some ways he was simply more of a child, for he smiled with pleasure to see that there was nowhere a nicking or even a turning of the sharp-ground edges. So he grasped the greasy black hair of Murray Quale and prepared to take his first scalp.

Something stopped him. It was not the consideration that the soul of a scalped warrior cannot leave the body but must rot away with the flesh; it was simply that he remembered the faces of Richard Lester and Maisry as, on that first night, they had watched him tearing at the roasted meat which they had given to him. White men, unless they had gone Indian-wild on the frontier, do not mutilate the dead. It seemed to Red Hawk that Maisry stood beside him in the cold and windy pass, watching everything he did with eyes as soft as those of a child, but recording forever.

Thereupon he simply drew the edge of the knife around the central section of the hair, in ceremonial fashion, and in a few words offered that untaken scalp to Sweet Medicine as a sacrifice.

Of the guns and ammunition of the dead man he took nothing, nor anything that was on his person, for the dead thing had grown unspeakably vile in the eyes of Red Hawk. As for the live stock it was a different matter. He took the mule and the two horses, so that, as he took up the trail of the White Horse once more, he now had a string of four animals.

The winter came on early that year. In October it was like December; in November it was like January. It seemed to him a special miracle when blindly marching south over the same route which he had followed the year before, he came again within view of the great horse, once more unattended by a herd. The whole body of tough mustangs which the White Horse had stolen from Murray Quale had drifted to one side or the other, worn out by the steadiness of the pursuit. There remained only the great leader himself, and once more the White Horse led him south to the Colorado.

How Red Hawk caught a wild horse in a cottonwood tangle and tamed and rode the brute, is a story too long to tell. But that tough roan carried his master over fifteen hundred miles, through the warmer south and back again into the freezing north, before on a March day, it dropped its head and could go no more.

99

Red Hawk resumed the way on foot. It would be unfair to say that he thought of surrendering. Fever maddened him with thirst and turned his brain astray until on a day he threw the ponderous weight of the rifle away from him. That brought him a little closer to starvation, but already he had starved until his cheeks clove like rough leather to his teeth.

In spite of fever and starvation, however, he kept to the trail of the White Horse, for the great stallion was no longer what he had been. If he needed less sleep than the man, he required several hours for grazing—particularly when he had to paw away the snow to get at his food. But those hours were never his, now that he had not the strength to burst away at a reaching gallop and put a few miles of security between him and this patient, dogging enemy. Fear had grown such a part of the great horse that he dared not snatch three mouthfuls without jerking up his head and study the wind and stare suspiciously all around him. If the man was but a shambling skeleton, the White Horse was hardly more.

As they entered the Blue Water Mountains, the veriest runt of a cow pony would have had speed enough to bring Red Hawk up with the stallion, so that he could at last use his rawhide lariat.

That lariat and his knife were the last of his possessions when he came to the last day. He had dug into the heaped snow on the windward side of a thicket and slept there for a few hours of wretched dreams. Then he dragged himself along the trail of the horse, over a ridge and down into a windless valley. The sun came up, strong and clear, and almost in a moment he could hear the lodged snow on the branches begin to fall. A few great storms might still be left in the skies, but the back of winter was breaking and the long thaw had begun.

It was a beautiful valley, and those who know the Blue Water Mountains can imagine how the slopes rose, so gigantic that the pine trees that struggled through the snow looked like a dark stubble. They will remember how the round lake, now glazed over with ice, lies in the bottom of the hollow.

Red Hawk, as he went down the hollow with knees unstrung by famine and the long labor, stared at the scene with bloodshot eyes. He knew, as though the voice of Sweet Medicine had sounded in his heart, that he had come to the end of his trail. There was no power in him to climb another ridge. He had felt a thousand times before that he was making his last march; but now there was a lump of ice in his vitals, and he was certain that his end was near.

That was why he felt no particular leap of joy through his body when he stole through the frozen bracken and came out on the shore of the lake, with the White Horse hardly ten strides away from him, breaking through the snow crust with strokes of his fore-hoofs and then tearing up with his teeth the long, brown, lank grasses that all summer long grew beside the water.

Little by little, Red Hawk worked his lariat into the coil, freed the noose, enlarged it, and began to prepare himself for the cast. His prayer was silence; and every breath he drew, to be sure, was a prayer. He felt that his arm was too weak for the throw; that he would be unable to succeed unless the Listeners Underground were good to him.

Then, taking a half-step forward, he hurled the noose. It was that half-step that warned the White Horse. That noise was a mere whisper, but it started the stallion away so that the noose, falling, merely whipped him across the withers and sent him into a frantic gallop right out across the face of the lake.

There was still strength enough in the horse to keep him

from slipping and falling. Though he skidded half a dozen times, he regained his control. He was almost across the lake when, with dying eyes, Red Hawk saw the monster disappear from view.

CHAPTER 17

RED HAWK saw two things that for an instant were dissociated in his mind; the disappearance of the horse and the leap of the crystal water. Only a moment later, he realized that the stallion must have broken through a flaw of the ice. Half running, half skating, with the length of the lariat snaking out behind him, the trailer saw the head of the White Horse, blackened with wetness, appear above the edge of the water, bobbing as though it were tossed by waves. When he came closer, he could see the reason for that swaying up and down, for the right foreleg of the stallion hung limp, and only with the left was he striking out. He swung a little to the side, as though through fear and to avoid the horrible nearness of the Man; but immediately he straightened out for the edge of the ice, though that was where Red Hawk awaited him.

All glory had gone out of the world; an endless age had passed since Red Hawk had first seen the White Horse racing on the plain. The white Indian was now a tottering old man who pulled on the rope to haul ashore an ancient horse whose backbone was lifting clear of the water, whose ribs stood out one by one, and whose hip bones were like great, blunt elbows trying to thrust through the skin.

He pulled until the White Horse, coming to the edge of

the ice, heaved up with a great effort and brought the fore-hoof heavily down on the rim. That effort to raise himself merely smashed the ice to pieces, so that Red Hawk shot feet first into the throttling coldness.

He came right up beside the struggling head of the stallion, and together they fought on towards the firm ground, out upon which Red Hawk climbed, the White Horse floundering after him on three legs.

But there was no joy in Red Hawk, no racing of the pulse as he saw his rope safely around the neck of the monster. His brain was like his body, numb and trembling; he had not even wit enough to turn a half-hitch around the trunk of a tree in order to hold his prize. Therefore, at the first lurch the rawhide burned through his grasp; and the White Horse drove away on three feet only, the right fore-leg dangling, flopping, until in the midst of tall saplings near by he slipped in the snow and went down.

Red Hawk, staggering in pursuit, now leaned a hand against a bending tree trunk and watched as the horse three times strove to rise. He could not bring himself clear, for the right foreleg was pinned beneath him. An inexpressible agony burned in the stallion's eyes, set his whole body shuddering.

There could be no doubt that foreleg was smashed to pieces. It seemed to the man that it was a story he had heard before, of how Red Hawk had pursued the White Horse, not contented with that glimpse of free beauty which roved the plains and climbed the mountains, until at last he put his rope on a broken and ruined white ghost. The illusion was so clear that he could almost breathe the acrid smoke of the fire in Spotted Antelope's lodge and hear the solemn voice of the old brave as he brought the tale to a moral end.

Red Hawk's own legs gave way under him until he

found himself sitting on a projecting root of the tree. A wind off the lake handled his wet body with fingers of ice. But his flesh could not be as cold as the heart in him. There was in him no further will to live.

Drowsiness began to work in his brain. He knew the meaning of that deadly sleepiness; but life had no savor nor worth, and sleep was better . . .

A blast in his very ears, like the thundering of many horns, roused him. It was the neighing of the White Horse, struggling to reach his feet again.

A smile twisted at Red Hawk's freezing face, for it seemed to him that the helpless stallion was not sounding that call to the whole world but only to rouse the one man who had managed to lay hand on him. Rouse him to what? Well, so that they might face death on their feet, perhaps.

He pushed himself up to his feet, tied the lariat about the tree. Going to the fallen horse, he put his hands under the animal's right shoulder, and heaved with all his might. Even that feeble assistance was enough to enable the White Horse to lunge to his feet; but in a stride, he had come to the end of the rope and was jerked about, facing it. After that he struggled no more.

Perhaps it was the agony of his injured leg that subdued him; perhaps the iron grip of the rawhide had convinced him. At any rate, he stood perfectly still while Red Hawk wormed his fingers up that dangling leg, reading every bone and joint and sinew to the knee, without finding a break.

Then an uncertain flame of hope wavered in the brain of Red Hawk; a hope that scarcely warmed his blood before it began to vanish. Gently he moved the stallion's leg forward and back. He pressed his ear against the wet shoulder of the horse to hear the grating of any broken bone, but he could make out nothing. The leg was sound! Clear to the top of the shoulder it was sound!

104

The only injury, therefore, must be to the shoulder nerve, for Red Hawk could remember that matchless healer, Lazy Wolf, speaking of such a thing. Sometimes it meant a ruined horse; sometimes the hurt might heal—if only the weight of the body could be taken from the leg so that it hung free, in a sling.

But a horse cannot stand indefinitely on three legs. Red Hawk stood before the head of the White Horse and looked into the unfathomable brightness and challenge of the beast's eyes. Something might still be done—if only wisdom would be given, to keep the clear flame of that spirit shining.

Red Hawk looked up to the sky and saw the slender tops of the saplings waving against it. That was what gave him his idea.

He set to work with a frantic haste. By the edge of the lake there were quantities of vines that climbed up among the lower branches of the trees, strong as supple ropes. He cut down a quantity of them, climbed some of the nearest saplings on either side of the horse, and fastened the vine-ropes near their tops. Afterwards, descending to the ground, he pulled down those trees until their heads were as close to the earth as his strength would bring them.

Some of the tips of the young pines brushed against the side of the White Horse; but still he remained motionless, his ears pricked, his head as steady as the pointing hand of a compass. It was as though he submitted in a spirit of jest, ready at any instant to leap away and snap the slender strength of the rope. But all the while hope grew strong and stronger in Red Hawk, until he forgot the weakness of body.

More than a score of those stubborn trees he bent before he tied strong withes, doubled and redoubled, from those on the right to those on the left and passed the improvised ropes under the body of the White Horse until they made an almost solid network. After that, first on this side and then on that, he cut the first withes which had drawn down the tops of the saplings towards the ground; and one after another, they gave the full strength of their recoil to lift the body of the stallion from the ground. Two still remained to be cut on either side when Red Hawk saw the feet of the White Horse lifted clear of the ground. Another and another—and on an even balance, the great horse swung cradled a foot above the snow!

Now there was hope indeed! Red Hawk found a quantity of dead brush and a number of dead stumps, not far away. A section of the sound rund from one of those stumps served him as a shovel to clear the snow away from beneath the horse. Then he found a piece of flinthard rock; and off to one side, with the butt of his knife he struck a shower of sparks into a little heap of powder-dry shavings and wood pulp until the tinder smoked and flamed. There was fire then, and plenty to feed it. There was food for the horse; he had only to kick away the surface snow, here and there, and harvest armfuls of the long grass.

There was even time, in the late afternoon, to think of his own trembling body. To that end, he whittled and notched a number of straight twigs, and made a series of strong little traps which he set along the runways which the rabbits had made through the snow among the trees. He baited the traps with a plentiful supply of seeds taken from the heads of the grasses.

Now he could afford time to make the sling that must support the leg of the White Horse; and in the dusk of the twilight he finished it so that it supported the loose leg at the elbow and at the knee, firmly.

There was barely light, now, for him to visit his traps, and in them find two winter-lean rabbits, already captured!

A ravenous hunger filled him, but still he dared not waste time on himself. He had to put up those rabbits, and with their shredded sinews he sewed up the rags of his deerskin shirt into the form of a large bowl which he stiffened around the edges with sections of supple branches fitted together.

With fine grass he then stuffed the chinks of the bowl and made the crude thing fairly watertight with a plastering of mud. It was by no means perfect. Water streamed through it in small spouts as he carried it from the lake to the White Horse. And for reward he was forced to stand until his arms were numb with fatigue before the wary stallion would deign to touch the surface of the water with his extended upper lip.

Afterwards, however, the horse drank deeply, while his half naked man-servant staggered back and forth between him and the margin of the lake. But Red Hawk was unconscious of the whipping cold. Sometimes, in his joy, he even laughed, on a note so strange that it startled his own ears.

About midnight he was able to think of himself. He roasted the flesh of the rabbits and devoured it—all save a few fragments which must be kept for a very definite purpose the next day. Afterwards, on a bed of soft branches which he had hewed down with the sword-like weight of his knife, he slept close to the fire—loose-bodied, sick with exhaustion, shuddering.

Once a soft sound aroused him. It was the whinny of the stallion; and as Red Hawk sprang up, he saw vague shapes disappear from the verge of the firelight and sink away among the trees. If the wolves began to haunt him, from this time on there would be small chance of trapping rabbits or any other prey. Then he remembered that the spirits had been kind to him, and with hope in his heart, he went back to sleep once more. Not until the cold of the morning wakened him to show him the last dying coals of his fire did he know anything further.

CHAPTER 18

It is not well for a horse to hang in a sling for twenty-four hours a day. Therefore, with painful care, Red Hawk built a solid platform of heavy branches, too thick for him to cut through with the knife, and therefore burned until they were of the right dimensions. When that platform was completed, it was of exactly the right height to permit the stallion to bear his own weight when he chose. Otherwise he could put his entire weight on the sling by the mere bending of his knees.

A storm began to scream on that second day, so Red Hawk built of pine branches a wind-break, twisting the branches between the thick standing saplings. When the edge of the wind was turned, he completed the building of a small lean-to. The main poles were up that first day; but it was not until a week later that he completed the thatching of the little structure on the top and on the sides. There was one small, rounded entranceway, and just to the side of that doorway he built a fireplace of stones.

Starvation threatened him during this time. His traps could still catch rabbits in plenty, but time after time the wolves and a few prowling coyotes emptied the traps of all but a few flying bits of fur. As for fish, he could see the big fellows swimming close to the surface, but on the few occasions when he hooked one on a thorn they easily broke

108

away again. So he made a long pole, with two short barbs in the sharpened end of it, and hardened that end in the fire. With that as a spear, he had fair success, throwing in some bits of frozen rabbit meat for bait, and then impaling the larger fish as they swarmed to eat.

Bringing forage to the White Horse required a considerable time, also, and the stallion had to be watered three times a day. But the greatest portion of time Red Hawk spent in carefully massaging the stallion's injured shoulder. He had found a spot, just above the shoulder bone, where the pressure of his fingers made the horse wince, and all the muscles about that place he massaged, day after day, for hours.

He had other things to do, such as weaving a clumsy, sleeveless jacket out of strips of the under bark of willows. It was not really warm, but it at least turned the edge of the cold March winds. Then he had to put up poles under the bent saplings which supported the weight of the White Horse. The stallion himself, even in these cramped quarters, began to grow sleek, and he no longer shuddered whenever the man came near him.

Yet it seemed to Red Hawk that the wary light never grew tame in the animal's eyes. Far more than that, he could hardly see any diminution in the sensitiveness of the sore place above the shoulder, as he bore in upon it with his finger tips. Every day he removed the leg from the sling, but every day it hung as loose and helpless as before, a dangling weight. Gradually, as the weeks went by, it began to shrink, particularly about the lower shoulder. The flesh grew flabby there, and he could feel the structure of the bone through the muscles. Therefore every day was filled with a recurrent misery.

Every day there also arose in Red Hawk a hope which was based upon what he had heard in his childhood from the old tellers of tales in the Cheyenne camp, when they discoursed wonderful stories of how men had tamed the beasts of the wilderness. The red-eyed ferret, blind with blood, had been the friend of men, it was said; even the wise and cruel grizzly had been at one time the pack-horse and protector of some friendless warrior, wounded and helpless. Therefore Red Hawk watched and waited for the moment when some light of playfulness might come into the eyes of the stallion—when at least he would take food from the hand.

But that time never came. The hour-long strokings with the hand, the infinite patience and gentleness of voice accomplished nothing, it seemed; and always there was that slight drawing back, as if rather in disgust than in fear, so that sometimes a savage anger burst up in the heart of Red Hawk and made him like a child, ready to destroy the thing for which he had worked so long.

Such was his misery in that cold camp that every day was like the step of a dying man, uphill, until he was awakened one night by a warm breath on his face, and dreamed that the White Horse was standing over him.

When he awakened, he heard the trees lashing. His whole body was hot. On the earth about him were whispering sounds of running water, and from the lake he heard the deep groaning of the ice. The great thaw had commenced. In that single night the lower slopes were turned from white to black; the forest became a marsh.

If spring had come there in the woods, it was already summer on the plains where the Cheyennes roved. Yet Red Hawk waited day after day, once every twenty-four hours releasing the injured leg from the sling and testing its power to uphold its own weight. But always without result.

For another whole month he told himself, from day to

day, that he had proved the case to the finish, and that this was the end. On the morrow he must put the White Horse out of this wretched, lame existence. But when the next day came he still postponed the killing.

For a whole month after the thaw, therefore, he waited; and on the thirtieth day he cut the network which had so long helped to support the body of the great horse. He also cut the sling that supported the leg, and sadly observed how the leg trailed down on the ground. Then, as he drew his knife, he wondered if he could find strength in his arm to strike the fatal blow, or with what ceremony this famous life ought to be brought to a close.

First, with the smoke of some sweet-smelling bark he purified the place and the horse and his own right hand. Then he threw up his arms to make a sacrificial prayer. At the flash of the raised knife, the White Horse wheeled suddenly away through the open gap where Red Hawk had torn down the southern wall of the tree-house, and he ran down the edge of the lake between the water and the brush.

With every step the beast staggered; yet it seemed to the incredulous eye of the man that it was not altogether the high-headed tossing of a three-legged horse. It seemed to him, actually, that the fourth foot was striking the ground.

Suddenly joy broke on him, blinded him; for the first time in his life, hope that was not for himself rushed through his heart like the spring wind over the cold mountains of winter. Among the trees he ran madly; through the brush he burst, heedless of the thorns that tore at his flesh with claws; and so came out on a wide meadow and into view of the White Horse, who was frolicking in the grass. It was true that four legs supported him, and that the right foreleg, though very feebly, helped to maintain the burden!

111

But the limping was no matter. The strength would return. The long-grown hoofs would wear down to the right dimensions, and the White Horse be king once more!

Red Hawk began to dance like a madman, shouting in such a way that a single yell made him hoarse. In his ecstasy he totally forgot that his rope was no longer on the neck of the stallion, until the White Horse swept away through a grove of trees.

Now, left alone, it seemed to Red Hawk that all the mountains drew suddenly nearer and looked down upon him. Or was it only that he looked into his own heart as he told himself that his vow, after all, had been accomplished. He had sworn that he would put his hand on the White Horse, and that he had accomplished. As for that other purpose of carrying the stallion back to Witherell and giving it as the marriage-price into the hand of the girl, that was not a part of his vow. It had not been properly recorded in the ears of Listeners Above or Underground.

There was no reason for him to return to the camp except to get a lariat, which would be useless to him now. So he turned his face immediately to the southwest and began his march through the Blue Water Mountains. He was sad, yet strange to say he was exalted. In him there was no sense of the time that had been wasted; rather, he felt that these days, of all his life, had been by far the most significant portion. To something he was infinitely nearer, though he could not find a name for it.

He went by slow marches, pausing to set traps for rabbits or birds, digging up roots here and there like a browsing bear. When at last he had advanced through the Blue Waters, and from a lofty peak looked over the foothills to the smoking plains beyond, it was near sunset time. He had filled his eyes with that sight, when the neigh of a horse rang through the pass behind him. No voice but one could send such echoes through his brain; and as he turned he saw the White Horse on a hillock in the middle of the pass, the glow of the sunset on him.

The sunset faded before the great horse moved.

It was a week later, far down on the edge of the plains where he had killed a mountain grouse and was roasting it, that he heard that whinny once more, near by. He saw that the stallion had come up out of the mouth of a draw. The morning sun burnished him; the morning wind blew out his mane and tail. But Red Hawk forgot to admire that beauty, as the tremendous certainty came home to him that he was being followed!

He forgot the good red meat which he needed so sorely, and hurried out toward the horse. From a distance he held out one hand, palm up, in the ancient gesture of friendship to man or to beast. But when he was near, the stallion left his stand like an arrow, to go winging out over the plain.

"He turns! He comes back! If he so much as turns his head, he is mine!" said Red Hawk to his soul.

Yonder, in the distance, the White Horse was indeed wheeling, sweeping back; charging with head stretched out and with flattened ears, and with mane lifted erect by the wind of that gallop as though it was the headdress of a chief. Every trace of limp, or even weakness, was gone from him. He planted his four hoofs and skidded to a halt, throwing up the clotted turf before him. He was not ten strides away, but Red Hawk folded his arms in the savage ecstasy of possession.

He raised his hand as though to address a chief in council. "You are mine," he said. "I let you wander for a while behind me; but when I wish, I shall put out my hand and take you!"

Then he turned his back and marched for three days across the prairies.

113

Sometimes the stallion was out of sight; sometimes he was a glimmering point on the horizon; but more often he was grazing near by. It was on the morning of the fourth day that he walked up to Red Hawk and looked the man in the eye.

What is it to strike a beast dead? What is it to ensnare the wild, living? What is it to wear them to a ghost of weakness and force them to surrender? All of these things are nothing to the joy that rioted in the soul of Red Hawk as he touched this glory that had freely come to him.

It was three days before he could sit on the back of the White Horse, but what did that matter? It was enough to see the beauty by the sheen of the dazzling sun or by the golden waves of firelight. It was enough to speak, and see that head turn, to hold out a hand and have this winged king come to him.

When he swung onto the stallion's back for the first time, the horse turned into a whip-snake of white silk that flung him headlong at the sky. But afterwards the White Horse came to inquire why he lay so long on the ground!

So, at the end of the third day, Red Hawk sat on the stallion's back, and the White Horse understood. There was no doubt of that, for first he walked, then he cantered, then he galloped, with his head turned a trifle as though to make sure that all went well with that weak, spindling, two-legged creature who was pegged on his back, clinging with blind hands to the flutter of the mane. And at last he raced at full speed, faster and faster, until it seemed to Red Hawk that he saw the wind go by in dark streaks.

There followed delirious days. That horizon which is set like a blue wall around the world was lifted. In a stride, in a gesture, so it seemed, Red Hawk could be over the rim of it on the back of the great horse. Hate could not pursue him; envy could never catch him; the White Horse was a throne from which he looked down happily upon the world.

CHAPTER 19

AFTER that, Red Hawk headed straight for Witherell. Even with this swift mount, the miles were long; but in the sunset of a certain day he came through the pass and looked down on the town, all its western windows filled with wavering golden light. Two things he saw like two well-known faces: the roof of the blacksmith shop, and the roof of Richard Lester's house. Then the White Indian went down the slope.

It was not easy to persuade the horse to go. Those thousand odors of ever-dreaded man thronged the air, and the strange sights and sounds of the village filled the White Horse with terror so that Red Hawk had to dismount and lead him by the mane.

They were on the edge of the town before they were noticed; then the whole populace turned out. Boys came first of all. They did not run at Red Hawk with loud jibes now. There was no flinging of stones. They scarcely seemed to notice the ragged misery of the patched skins in which he was dressed. Instead, they held back to a distance, with muffled exclamations.

Women and men came running also. They filled in the sides of the street, and a clamoring began from which the White Horse shrank closer and closer to his master; and the more he cowered beside Red Hawk, the more the murmuring rose.

Red Hawk could not pick out many individual voices, but he afterward remembered two things—how he went past the lofty figure of Wind Walker, who stood with folded arms, his neighbors giving him plenty of room on either side; and how Sam Calkins bawled out, "There he comes! I knew he'd do it. A blacksmith is the boy for a hard job, every time. Brains'll take more than horses!"

Now Red Hawk was in front of Richard Lester's house, where he saw the lawyer lying in a chair that was half a bed, placed on the front veranda, facing to the south and west as though to enjoy the last heat of the day.

The girl whipped out the door, then stood with one hand gripping the edge of it as Red Hawk turned in at the gate. He stared ahead of her, and then aside at the stallion. He could not tell which was the greater, the painful thought of surrendering the horse, or the pleasure at the knowledge that her heart had been great enough to ask for that king of the prairies as her marriage-price. Then he walked up the gravel of the path, with the White Horse crowding at his heels.

Now he stood at the bottom of the steps. The girl was standing as one enchanted. Now he was lifting his right hand in the greeting.

There was a ceremonial solemnity in his manner that had hushed the voices of the crowd following him, and that was why every one for a great distance could hear him so perfectly as he said:

"This is the price you named. I give you the White Horse, and I take you as my squaw. Bring a rope so that you may lead him. Then come with me to my lodge."

There followed a moment of pause. In it he seemed to see the girl's widening eyes. Then from behind him, up and down the street, laughter burst out like water from a broken dam; mirth and mockery that screamed in shrill trebles and thundered in deep bass notes.

The uproar made the White Horse flash about, shouldering heavily against his master. Red Hawk turned also, to glance over his shoulder at the crowd. When he looked toward the house again, the girl was gone and Richard Lester was rising from his chair. He walked slowly down the steps, leaning on a cane, and Red Hawk saw the face of a sick man. There was no laughter about Lester as he took the hand of Red Hawk.

"Come inside with me," he said.

"The White Horse would break through the wooden floors," said Red Hawk, "and I cannot leave him. Where is Maisry? Has she gone to say good-bye to her mother? Has she gone to make her pack? I want her to come to me with empty hands."

"You'll see Maisry. I promise you that," Lester assured him. "But come with me around to the back of the house, out of sight of these foolish people!"

He led the way to the rear, but still the laughter washed up and down the street in waves. Inside the house, Red Hawk heard the sharp and angry outcry of Mrs. Lester.

Richard Lester sat on a sawbuck beside the woodpile, his hands folded over the head of his cane. The White Horse was still shouldering close to his master, while the happy eye of Red Hawk roved over the golden western sky, and over the deep blue of the hills, contentedly. It seemed to him a proper moment for his woman to come out and put her hand in his and follow him.

"This matter of a marriage-price—and my daughter," said Lester. "What is that about, Red Hawk?"

"She has told you, of course," answered he. "I know that among the whites a girl is not sold as among the Indians; but she gives herself away for whatever she pleases. I have heard that some give themselves even for bright beads. But

117

Maisry is not like others. She has the proud heart of a Cheyenne. She would not sell herself for a sparrow, but for an eagle. So fortune was kind to me, and I have brought her the eagle out of the air."

He smiled happily at Lester, and the lawyer, half frowning, answered:

"Do I understand, Red Hawk, that you have been trailing the White Horse for these two years on account of my girl? Oh, we've heard the tales of you in the plains and in the mountains. I hear that the Blackfeet have buried the hatchet and made peace with the Cheyennes, because of you. But you have been hunting the White Horse all on account of my daughter?"

Red Hawk's conscience troubled him a little. He had to take thought for a moment before he could answer:

"Well, there is another reason. When I saw him, I could not take him out of my eye. But who am I to hunt down the White Horse that whole tribes have failed to take? It was only good luck, and much waiting, that gave him to me."

"Maisry!" called Lester. "You must come out here, my dear!"

The kitchen door opened, and Mrs. Lester's excited face appeared. "She'll do no such thing!" she cried. "Richard Lester, what are you thinking of?"

"There's a mystery here," said the lawyer. "Maisry, you'll have to come!"

And suddenly the girl was hurrying down the steps, throwing off her mother's hand.

CHAPTER 20

It seemed to Red Hawk that he could see the girl's whole nature as she came down the steps toward him. Where her will was bent, there was no strength in the world that could restrain her. An ecstasy came over him. He started to proclaim himself in a chant that rushed from his lips, crying out:

"I am the Red Hawk. Look at me! Wonder at me! I am that man who saw the White Horse blow over the green earth like a cloud across the sky. He ran with the wind, and I walked; but my steps were longer than his, and I touched him. He ran, but I stepped over the mountains and caught him in my hand. I looked from the mountain top and the White Horse moved through the valley like the image of a cloud in still waters. I reached down and caught him.

"*Ah-hai!* Do you see him? Is there truth in the tongue of Red Hawk, or is he a double-speaker? He brings the White Horse back. He puts him in the hand of the girl. He closes her fingers around him. He makes the White Horse belong to her.

"He is yours! Take him. Sit on his back while I walk beside you. Come away with me till we see the smoke going up from the lodges of the Cheyennes. They are my people. They see your face and they laugh with happiness. They fill the pots with back fat and buffalo meat. They are feasting and singing.

"Give me your hand. Let me put you on the back of the

White Horse, and he will carry you over the edge of the world and back again to me."

The stallion, as his master walked back and forth, chanting, moved restlessly. Now he galloped to the end of the yard; now wheeled and flew back to stand beside Red Hawk, now shook his head as though to deny the words that were spoken. At the end, Red Hawk made a step forward, holding out his hand to the girl.

The mother cried out in a shrill voice of denial, but that was nothing to Red Hawk. What mattered to him was that the girl made no gesture to meet him.

The hand which he extended to her turned to lead and fell back to his side. Then he heard Richard Lester saying: "What is it, Maisry? You must tell me what this is all about?"

"There is something," she answered. "Go inside with Mother and see if you can quiet her. I'm not going to run away, if that's what she's afraid of. And I must find out what Red Hawk is thinking about. I must be alone with him in order to find out."

"You're right," said Lester, and walked past her into the house.

The kitchen door closed. The sharp voice of the wife and the deeper, quieter voice of Lester trailed forward through the house and were silent.

"Now, Red Hawk," said the girl. "Will you tell me why you thought that the White Horse was a marriage-price for me—as you call it?"

She spoke with the gentleness, he felt, of one who does not wish to deceive, but who would make everything clear, even to the mind of a child.

He said, sadly, "Even the good and the brave forget. One winter may cover a deep trail. But I remember that when I was a slave in this camp, one day I was free again. I went to the creek and washed the filth of the slavery away from my body. I came down to a place where I heard voices, and one of them was yours. Two men were with you. Both asked for you to come to their lodges, and then you made a choice. You told them that you would follow the man who brought you the White Horse. And that is why the White Horse is here!"

She had uttered a faint cry before he came to the last words. She was saying, over and over:

"It was but a joke, Red Hawk! It was but a joke. It was a way of saying that I liked them both, but that I wouldn't marry either of them. It was a way of saying that I cared for neither Jeremy nor Joe enough to marry. It was only an extravagant way of talking. It was only a joke, Red Hawk!"

"*Hai!*" said Red Hawk, softly. He moved his arms as if to draw a robe about him. "It was a joke. Ought I to laugh? I cannot laugh. I am only a Cheyenne, and the whites laugh at me. Even the women laugh at me."

"I do not laugh at you," she told him, earnestly. "I'm sick at heart!"

"The White Horse is not what you want, then. And Red Hawk you don't want. What is he? He is not a chief. Maisry waits for a great man of her own people; and Red Hawk is but a dirty Indian!"

"If I had known what you were going through for my sake," she said, "I would have— No, there is nothing that I could have done. My father is very ill, Red Hawk. I must find a husband who can take care of him, and of my mother and of me."

"To look on the face of a mother-in-law is not permitted. It is a bad thing!" said Red Hawk. "But I can find a lodge for them, and another for you and me. I am a good hunter, and there will always be meat for the pot. And you will have the White Horse! *Hai!* Think of how he will put his head through the entrance flap in the morning and tell us that the sun is rising!"

"Let me try to explain," she continued. "I want you to know, exactly. I couldn't speak of it to another person, but I must tell you, Red Hawk. I've never known another being who was more to me than— No, what I must tell you is that my father needs the care of very wise doctors. He has to go to a different part of the world, where even the wind at night is never cold. Do you understand? I must have money to take care of him—a great deal of money!"

"I shall take the three of you so far south that we will be inside the lodge of the sun," he told her.

He went close and stood over her. "Why do you put up words for me to jump over?" he said. "If I went out and caught the White Horse, do you think that the talking of a squaw will hold me away? Don't speak to me like a girl, but like a man—honestly, so that I can understand you. Women talk over their shoulder. They run away, and their eyes ask a man to follow them. But I shall not follow you like a foolish boy. Will you talk to me as men talk?"

The White Horse suddenly tried to pass between them. Red Hawk put out his hand on the muzzle of the great stallion, and for a moment the White Horse amused himself by tossing the hand up and down.

"I'll try to talk as you wish," said the girl.

"Tell me, then, if you feel what I feel, that it is happiness to be near you and sickness to be away; that to be near you is like eating when I am very hungry, and to be away is like having a full belly that loathes food. It is strength to be close to you, and weakness to be away from you. Have you felt like that? Say quickly as a man would say!"

"Never before," said the girl. "But when you brought

122

the White Horse back with you—now I know what it is. I shall be unhappy when you go away again."

"That is good!" said Red Hawk. "*Hai!* When you say that, I step to the top of a mountain and see the world! I want to talk more about you. Even if there were more light, I should not be able to see you more clearly, because my eyes have moved over you little by little, slowly, as the sun moves, eating up the shadow. My eyes have gone over your face, so that even when I was far away your lips and your eyelids must have felt a warmth as I thought of you.

"Now listen to me. I am not a great chief among my people. I am not even a warrior to sit in the council, because I shrank from the sacrifice of blood. You see that I have put all my heart nakedly before you, as a child is naked in the arms of its mother. But still I have friends in the tribe. There are people who love Red Hawk and wait for him. My father sits with his head covered, and he hopes for my voice. I see the white lodges and the green plains, and the horses grazing, sleeking their sides with good pasture.

"I have been far away from all of these things, and I have been hungry for them. Do you understand?"

"I understand," said a broken voice.

"*Hai! Ah-hai!*" exclaimed Red Hawk. "Now you understand truly. You are sad. But if I can make you sad, then I can also make you happy."

"Yes," said the girl. "It is true."

"It is dark now," said he. "But here is my hand, close to the nose of the White Horse. I shall not touch you, Maisry; but if you put the tip of a finger against my hand, then you are mine as much as though you had lived a year in my lodge!"

He heard vague, faint sounds of grief in her throat. Then she said:

"I have given myself away to another man."

He caught hold of the White Horse's mane and clung to it.

"Jeremy Bailey," she said, "is rich enough to take care of all of us. I have given myself away to him. In another month I shall marry him."

He waited, unable to speak. At last he could say:

"So! I have been away hunting for a long time. And the old trails are covered so that my feet cannot find them again. Maisry, farewell!"

It was so dark, now, that he could only make out the glimmering of her face, but as he walked around the side of the house, with the White Horse behind him, he could hear a sound of grief coming from her. Very subdued it was, as though she were afraid that some one asleep might be wakened.

CHAPTER 21

RED HAWK knew that he was about to die. He was enmeshed in such a net that he could not possibly escape from the toils; and even if escape were possible, it seemed to him that there was no worth in existence. As he walked slowly down a by-way of the town of Witherell, it was merely the means of a quick release from this living misery that he thought about.

Far away, he heard the voice of Richard Lester, high-pitched, repeating his name in a piercing call. Well he knew that that man had enough kindness in him to regret that even a white Indian had been involuntarily deceived; but there was nothing in the power of words to relieve Red Hawk's mind. He was caught between two irresistible hands and crushed.

The lane he followed brought him to the side of the central square, so that he could now hear the tumult in the saloons. Each throat opened its outcry on a separate note, as the swinging doors at the entrance vibrated to and fro. Inside he could see men in skin caps, in felt hats, in sombreros; men in woven cloth or deerskins, who went around the square locked arm in arm, staggering, dead drunk. Now two groups stuck together, and instantly the men had fallen to the ground in couples, wrestling, cursing. Then knives began to flicker.

Spectators poured out from the saloons and stood about, making no attempt to intervene. They cheered on the combatants, as though it had been dogs which struggled on the ground.

Then there was a scream, a long, high-drawn death note that might have been from either a man or a woman, because there was nothing but the last agony in it. And the grinding of the knife against bone and through tender flesh as it found the life.

Red Hawk struck his hands against his ears, but could not shut out the last of that yell. He turned back across an open field, walking with no strength in his knees, and repeating in his mind that he was caught between two hands and crushed. Among the Indians he could be what? A man of some dignity and importance, perhaps, because he had caught the White Horse. But no matter what his deeds might be, the old shame of his failure in the medicine lodge would cling to him, and the medicine men and certain of the older warriors would always feel that the mere sight of him was a bane and a frightful example for the rising youth of the Cheyennes.

But if he were not to live among the Cheyennes, how could he exist with the whites of Witherell? If he could endure their brutality, he still could not withstand their mocking laughter.

He looked up, and the white faces of the stars struck a mortal cold through his soul; he looked down, and the darkness rose out of the ground and covered his mind. So, with the White Horse following him, he found himself at the verge of a small hollow through which a rivulet twisted, and by the edge of the running water there was a shack no larger than the lodge of an Indian, with one dim light shining through the window.

At first the place dawned on his brain like a dream that is being repeated with a familiar expectancy of something to come. It was only after a long moment that he remembered that this was the house of Marshall Sabin, whom the Cheyennes called Wind Walker. The instant he realized that, he felt that he understood why his feet had been led to the place. The thing was clear in his mind now. When a man is caught in a trap, it is best to keep fighting to the last, and so win a quick death. What death could be quicker and surer than for him to stand alone in front of Wind Walker, who had faced the chosen Cheyenne warriors three and four at a time and had left dead men behind him?

As for the chance of reward, if fortune were willing to favor him, and lay the Wind Walker dead at his feet, then indeed he would be able to return to the tribe with all the omissions of his past forgiven and forgotten. He would become the hero of the nation. Running Elk would have to regard his medicine with awe, and Dull Hatchet would be forced to admit him to the council.

He whispered a farewell to the White Horse, when he was close to the house; and took his last look at the stallion, more by touch of hand than by eye. Then he went on to the window. When he came close to it, he could understand why the light had streamed from it with such a dull ray, because the window was simply an oiled tissue and not glass at all. It was impossible for him to spy on the man inside without breaking the membrane; and that sound would, of course, be ample warning to Wind Walker, even if his favoring spirits had not already told him that an enemy was near!

Red Hawk went to the door, tried the latch with a soft hand, and flung the door suddenly wide open. He saw Wind Walker rise from a small table in the middle of the room, where he had been reading a book. With one hand the white man gripped the lamp, as if ready to dash it to the ground and give himself the protection of darkness. With the other hand he leveled a revolver at the door.

"Wind Walker!" called Red Hawk, using the Indian name, but speaking in English. "Do you hear me? I am Red Hawk. I have come to fight with you, and to see which of us is to die and which of us has the stronger medicine. I come with no gun; with only a knife. Are you ready to face me?"

Sabin, when he heard his name called out, at first lifted the lamp higher to throw more light on the threshold. Now he stepped back, letting his revolver fall down the length of his arm.

"Well," said Sabin, "come in peace, Red Hawk. No matter how you may happen to leave! Show yourself."

It was true that if he entered the room the white man might tilt up the muzzle of his revolver and make an end of one more Cheyenne; but Red Hawk did not hesitate. Great men of war were apt to fight fairly; and at any rate Wind Walker was so certain to conquer that he would hardly take an advantage, for that would give the kill no savor to him. For these reasons, Red Hawk stepped fearlessly upon the threshold and then into the room. He held the knife in his hand and now he cast it, in an access of desperate confidence, upon the floor.

"There is my knife," he said, "and here am I!"

He saw the muzzle of the revolver tilt upwards a little, as if an involuntary twitch of the muscles had stirred it. Then it hung down idly again; and presently Wind Walker put the gun back on the table beside the book which he had been reading. All this while he was taking hold of Red Hawk with his eyes, and Red Hawk, in turn, had a chance to glance about the room.

It was as simple a place as could be built with logs by two men in a pair of days. Mud had been used to stop, or partially stop, the gaps between the roughly-faced logs. For furnishings there was a bunk built against the wall, with a few blankets tossed carelessly on top of it, and no sign of even a pallet of straw.

Some clothes hung from pegs. A rifle, with a powderhorn hung to it, leaned in a corner beside a saddle that was suspended by one stirrup. Until one faced the fireplace, that was all that was to be seen, except for a small box or trunk piled with books.

But the fireplace itself was what took the major part of Red Hawk's attention. Not with its size or the three small pots that stood beside its crane, but because from a rawhide thong across the front of the hearth, as high as a man's head, there hung more than a score—yes, or even thirty, long black tresses of hair, with what seemed decaying rags of cloth attached to the bottoms of them. Whenever Wind Walker laid wood on his fire, whenever he bowed over the hearth to arrange the pots, he passed under the line of Cheyenne scalps.

Such trophies Red Hawk had seen by scores in the camp of the Cheyennes, and yet this sight sickened him, and not alone with grief for the losses of his own people.

He had noted these things with one swing of his eyes around the room; and he could give all of his heed now to the huge man who faced him. It seemed to him that he had never seen Wind Walker before, neither in the street of Witherell nor in the blacksmith shop of Sam Calkins. He seemed larger than ever, although he was stooped a little forward, in an attitude of readiness. His hair was not gray, but half white and half black, in streaks. In a sense, he seemed older; but his face was as timeless as a rock. He was saying:

"You're the renegade white that can't live with your own kind. You prefer the dog-eating Cheyennes."

Said Red Hawk, simply: "Is it for that reason that you hate my tribe, Wind Walker? Well, a fat dog makes a very good feast in the middle of winter, some men say. But I have never tasted the flesh. We have been through no great hungers during the time of my life."

"Dog-eaters or rat-eaters, you're all of a kind!" said Wind Walker, harshly. "But how does it happen that one of the gang is willing to step out in the open and fight like a man? Can you tell me that?"

"There are many braves among the Cheyennes," said Red Hawk, "who are not afraid to meet you."

"You lie!" said Wind Walker. "They run away from me like antelope."

Red Hawk threw up his head and flushed. "Why do you say the thing that is not true?" he demanded. "Here you see me, who never won a man's name among the Cheyennes; and yet even without a name I am not afraid to face you, Wind Walker."

"You lie again!" said Sabin. "You're white about the mouth with fear."

Red Hawk sighed. "It is true that my heart is cold," he

129

said. "But nevertheless I am here."

"You can't lift my hair, Red Hawk," said Sabin, easily. "It's not in the books that you can handle me. You'll win no great name from me, my lad. You'll get no more than a little inheritance of cold earth to stop your mouth and eyes for the rest of time. But by the eternal God, I've half a mind to let you go! I hunt the red Cheyennes for the sake of a woman whom they murdered, boy. There's nothing in me against a poor, deluded fool of a white lad that they've raised according to their lights."

"I know your squaw," said Red Hawk.

"You *know* her? You were hardly born when she died!"

"She has spoken a word to me out of the ground nevertheless," said Red Hawk.

The White Horse neighed anxiously outside the door, and then thrust his magnificent head through the opening and looked after his master.

"Do you see?" said Red Hawk. "I sacrificed a good horse to her ghost, and her spirit gave me fortune so that I caught you the White Horse."

"So it was you who laid that offal on her grave?" exclaimed Wind Walker, his voice rising to a thunder. He took a deep breath, suddenly, and controlled himself.

"Now, my lad," said he, "I think I understand you. You've come here to have it out with me, and so be able to ride back in a glory with the White Horse and my scalp. But you can't win. I'm not fool enough to fight with knives against a young wildcat; and you'd be a fool to fight me with guns, because I've lived with nothing but guns for twenty years. Do you hear me? Walk out the door, then, Red Hawk, and thank your spirits for the life that hasn't leaked out through a hole in your skin. Be off with you, lad!"

"Give me the small gun and take the rifle for yourself. We shall fight like that," said Red Hawk.

130

"D'you like the rifle better?" asked Wind Walker. "Take it, then."

The stallion whinnied as Red Hawk, without waiting for a second invitation, hurried to the wall and caught up the rifle. Sabin at the same time picked the revolver from the table. He said:

"Keep that rifle no lower than at the ready. If you begin to drop the muzzle at me till we've had a signal, I'll split your skull wide open between your blue eyes, Red Hawk. But I'll give you a last chance. I tell you now that at a range like this, I can't miss you. If we fight, you're dead. Lad, get out of the house and go back to the tribe! There are still enough red Cheyennes left for me."

"I have prayed to the Listeners Above and the Listeners Underground," said Red Hawk. "If they give me a victory it is very well; but if I die, I am only leaving a dark life."

"Damn the Listeners Above and Underground, when I have a loaded gun in my hand!" said Marshall Sabin. "There's your horse, flickering his nostrils and ready to whinny again. There's the signal for us to fire, when he neighs. And God help your rotten young soul!"

They faced one another in silence, the rifle at the ready, the revolver hanging straight down in Sabin's hand. It seemed to Red Hawk that Wind Walker was leaning a little farther forward, peering as though he saw in the face of Red Hawk a familiar landscape.

Then Red Hawk felt, rather than heard, the vibrating neigh of the stallion, and he jerked up the butt of the rifle to fire. He saw the revolver flash to a level, the muzzle of it tipped up as it spat fire; and the red streak of the flame seemed to explode through his whole brain, followed by darkness.

He found himself falling. The floor rushed up against his eyes and struck his entire body, heavily. And as he lay

131

still, he wondered that he was not dead. It was as though the blow of a club and the stroke of a knife had fallen upon his head at the same instant.

Wind Walker was coming. He had to rise and face death. He had to bring life back into his limbs for a final struggle. He saw the great moccasins striding toward him. He could see the powerful legs as high as the bulge of the calves. And suddenly it came to him that the gods of the white man must love this warrior; they had entrusted victory in his hands!

The big feet paused near him. He knew that the monster was bending above him. Red Hawk gathered himself through a tenth part of a second for the final effort. Then he thrust himself up with his left hand. His right caught up the gleaming length of his knife, and he drove it right at the breast of Wind Walker.

He had one glimpse of hope. Then, with a sidesweep of his revolver, Wind Walker struck the knife out of Red Hawk's grasp. It fell with a shiver of steel against the floor.

Still the final bullet did not crunch through Red Hawk's body and bones. He got to his feet, swaying. Death was right there before him, a glimmering light on the barrel of the revolver. It would strike him in the belly through the tender flesh. He could see that from one eye; the other was blinded with the blood that flowed from the wound in his scalp. He folded his arms and stood fast, as a helpless man should do, facing death with dignity. He hoped that when the gun crashed he would not fall writhing on the floor. He prayed that no screams of agony would tear through his locked teeth.

"You sneaking Cheyenne snake!" shouted Wind Walker, and stepped in with all his weight behind a driving fist. The blow caught Red Hawk well on the side of the chin, and hurled him sidelong into a second darkness.

CHAPTER 22

RED HAWK awakened with the cold of wind and water in his face, for he lay in grass wet with dew, and a breeze chilled him.

He sat up. The black, squat outline of Wind Walker's house stood before him, thrusting its sharp back up among the stars. The White Horse stood over him without grazing; and the gleam of something above the top of the grass proved to be his own long knife, which had been thrust into the ground beside him. Yet it was no dream that he had confronted Wind Walker in his own lodge, for when he felt a fiery thrust of pain through his head and lifted his hand, he found that the entire side of his head was bathed with blood.

Gradually exploring with the tips of his fingers, he could understand. The bullet from Wind Walker's gun had not driven through his head between the eyes. It had merely cut the flesh across his temple, and so glanced back along his skull, with impact enough to knock him down. Then he remembered what had followed. Far more strange than all else was the fact that Wind Walker had spared a Cheyenne life and had flung the limp body on the grass outside his lodge. Yet one more scalp could have hung to dry at his fire, and for an extra prize, here was the White Horse to carry the great warrior to his next battles! The slayer somehow seemed far more terrible because for once he had chosen to be merciful.

There was no need for haste as Red Hawk traveled out

from Witherell. At the grave of Wind Walker's squaw he stopped and listened in vain for the voice that had sounded in his mind before. Then, slowly, he moved back across the plain, pausing for several days at a pool where he could manage to spear fish.

When he reached the camp of the Cheyennes, the wound across the side of his head had closed. He so gauged his approach that he would not enter the camp until dark. Therefore he rode the White Horse at a walk, when he was still at a considerable distance, waiting for the sun to sink.

But he had forgotten how at this season of the year the boys from the camp would be sure to ride far afield, like war-scouts; and they stormed out at him from behind a hillock, a yelling swarm, their little ponies at full strain, the turf hurtling above their heads in lumps, like dark birds dancing in the air.

They came close up to him, while with voice and hand he was barely able to keep the stallion from bolting. One by one, the screeching youngsters flashed past him, each making a motion as if to shoot with the bow as he darted by Red Hawk.

Half of that stream of wild Cheyennes then poured away toward the camp to give the tidings; the other half whirled in a vast pool around Red Hawk. They yelled and screeched their praises while they raced their horses. But all of this mattered little or nothing to him. Indian boys are unhampered spirits; but what would their fathers and their older brothers do about the returning renegade who had not dared to endure the blood-sacrifice?

He had his answer in the red heart of the sunset time, as he drew near to the camp and saw a stream of warriors, skirted around by a swarm of boys as they came galloping out toward him. At the head of all, making his pony race at full speed, was Standing Bull. Red Hawk knew him by the war-cry that he sounded, and understood by that token than neither Dull Hatchet nor Running Elk had chosen to join in the reception. Neither the war chief nor the medicine man had come, for if either of them had been present the rest of the tribe would have held back. The most important faces had been turned away from him, but there was solace in those that remained. For to the right and left of Standing Bull, and far behind him, he could mark from a distance the braves of great and respected importance. He could tell them by their headdresses, by the horses which he had not forgotten. And as they came closer, he could distinguish their shouts, and last of all, their faces.

If the leaders of the Cheyennes had not come out to him, the rank and file of the warriors had not hesitated on that account. Standing Bull with one arm raised in welcome and in salute, made a swift circle around the White Horse, the war-yell screeching out of his throat until the White Horse in a frenzy reared and spun about on his hind legs.

At that sight all the other Cheyennes shouted and came pouring in.

Standing Bull took charge. He went ahead of his friend and ordered the circle to widen. He struck at horses with his whip to make them move. He thundered commands to clear the way. Nevertheless, the warriors rushed enthusiastically close to the stallion, until the White Horse suddenly took matters into his own control by making a furious charge, first to the right and then to the left, ready with his teeth and his hoofs to clear room.

With laughter and shouting, the Cheyennes dodged the charges. So the troupe passed into the camp.

On the verge of the camp was Lazy Wolf, smoking a short-stemmed pipe such as the whites prefer, and waving a staff in greeting. The Blue Bird was behind her father, waving, laughing.

135

Above all the other outcries Red Hawk could hear a steady chant that never ended as one voice after another cried: "The White Horse! The White Horse!"

Were they welcoming him, or only the "medicine" horse?

He had no difficulty in finding the lodge of Spotted Antelope. The crowd had formed a living alley, fencing in the way to the natural goal of his home-coming; and now, at the end of it, he saw the lodge of his foster-father. The entrance flap was open, but no one stood in front of the tepee; a sure sign that he was waited for within. So he rode on through the tumult, keeping his eyes straight before him, as in duty bound, and pretending to see no one.

When he dismounted and stepped inside the lodge, the White Horse crowded his head and shoulders after him through the entrance-flap. And then Red Hawk saw Spotted Antelope, looking aged and drawn and gray of skin. But there was no sign of Bitter Root, and by that he knew well that she had died.

Afterwards, he was alone with his father as much as could be, since the White Horse would not leave his place in the entrance and the feet of men and women and children could be seen thronging outside the lodge to view the great stallion close up. Against the flood of noise that still poured around the tepee the two men spoke at intervals, with long silences between. The flame of the central fire threw up waverings of light across the neatly sewn skins of the lodge. These skins were newly tanned, and yet Red Hawk was told that Bitter Root had died almost two years before.

There was an explanation when Bending Willow, the wife of Standing Bull, entered the lodge carrying a pot from the mouth of which streamed the savors and steam of

136

broiled buffalo meat. She placed the pot over the fire and went out, without speech.

"She?" said Red Hawk, lifting his finger.

"She has been like a daughter in my lodge," said the old man. "And Standing Bull has been as a son.

"Now tell me every step that the White Horse made across the plains and through the mountains," he commanded. He leaned back and stretching out his hands, not toward the fire but toward the warmth and brightness of the glory of his foster son. "But first," he said, "tell me what made the wound that is on your head."

"Wind Walker," said Red Hawk.

The Cheyenne was old, but now he leaped to his feet with a sudden agility. "Wind Walker!" he cried, and clapped a hand over his gaping mouth.

"Yes," said Red Hawk. "He fought with me. His bullet knocked me down, and afterwards he could have taken my life; but he threw me outside his lodge."

"You were in his lodge?" cried the old man. "You went into his lodge?"

"Yes," said Red Hawk. "I went inside his lodge to kill him or—"

"*Hai!*" cried Spotted Antelope. "You to kill Wind Walker? Listen to me! If you were to kill him, your bones would rot with unhappiness; your hair would fall from your head. You would lose the use of tongue and death would be close to you!"

Red Hawk listened with perfect bewilderment. "But why should that be?" he demanded. "What spirit has told you these things?"

But his foster father began to stare straight before him at nothingness, and now seemed incapable of either speech or hearing.

137

CHAPTER 23

It was clear that whatever Spotted Antelope saw, no questions would draw out his vision into words. Therefore his foster son was still.

A moment later, the voices of Lazy Wolf and Standing Bull called outside the lodge. With a gesture, Red Hawk brought the White Horse into the great tepee, and with another signal made him lie down like a dog on the ground. But his head remained nervously high, his eyes shining with more than the light of the fire which was reflected in them.

The two visitors, as they entered, paused for a long moment to stare at the horse before they sat down. Then all four sat in a circle, smoking a ceremonial pipe. Red Hawk, sitting close to the stallion, kept his left hand on the sheen of the hard muscles of the animal's neck, where it arched close to the head, and from time to time he tangled affectionate fingers in the White Horse's forelock. It seemed to him that there was now enough in his tepee to fill the heart of any man—two friends, his foster father, and the great horse. Yet his pleasure was as melancholy as some remembered happiness. They might have been ghosts who sat about and smiled at him, asking questions. He narrowed his eyes, in order to pierce into their minds and realize to the full this sun of friendship which was playing upon him. But nothing could lift the shadow from him or make them seem real.

What amazed and hurt him most of all was that he perceived everything with new eyes. Lazy Wolf began to look like a fat and lazy vagabond, with yellow tobacco stains in the gray of his curling beard. Spotted Antelope was a death's-head, over whose skull the skin was drawing tighter and tighter. The film of age covered his eyes, except when a frenzy lighted them from within, as when he had seen some warning vision of Wind Walker just now. And even Standing Bull had been new-made by the touches of the last three years, for the frown was permanently gathering between his eyes, and deep lines drew down past the corners of his mouth. His eyes flashed from moment to moment, as though he hunted on the warpath.

That sick man in the town of Witherell, with his lofty brow and gentle expression, was hardly stronger than a woman; but with the hand of the mind, perhaps, he could accomplish more than all of the men of the Cheyenne tribe.

However, the moment that thought formed in Red Hawk's mind he forced himself away from it. He summoned his spirits; he tried to forget the ache in his heart and to make these faces a little more real than the images that drifted up in his mind with the rising smoke of the fire.

He began to talk of the thing that they wished to hear; of the famous hunt for the White Horse. Yet he had hardly started the narrative when the voice of a crier went ringing through the camp. It paused not far away to shout the tidings.

Running Elk, the medicine man, and Dull Hatchet, the war chief, were together giving a feast in the lodge of the war chief. To that feast were invited all the important men of the tribe; the name of Standing Bull came early in the list, and that of Lazy Wolf also appeared, no matter how unpopular he might be with both of the Cheyenne leaders. Last of all, the crier chanted out the name of Spotted Antelope.

The four men in the lodge looked at one another listening, incredulous, unable to believe that the name of the returned wanderer had not been called.

"Well," said Standing Bull, as the fullness of the insult became more apparent to him, "I shall stay here. I could not now eat the food that is cooked in the tepee of Dull Hatchet."

Lazy Wolf raised a hand of warning. "You've quarreled with Dull Hatchet once before," he said, "and for a whole year you were not asked to join a single important war party. I know what it means to you to lose chances to lift hair or horses and risk your own scalp into the bargain. As for me, I am going to this feast; and you are coming with me. Spotted Antelope, come along with us. When the chief of the tribe calls us, it is a command. We'll be back to see you before long, Red Hawk."

Red Hawk, however, was suddenly seeing the truth as if from a great height. The days that were to come scattered before him like so many faces, although far away. Again he had that strange sense of a remembered thing, as though all the years of his life he had known that his doom was in the scarred and ugly face of Dull Hatchet. There could be no clearer way for the war chief and the medicine man to tell him that no matter how the younger men and women of the Cheyennes looked up to the captor of the White Horse, the great and important heads of the tribe had not forgotten that Red Hawk had failed in the blood sacrifice of the initiation.

And Red Hawk, as he watched his friends move out from the tent, felt that he was looking at them for the last time. Standing Bull stood for an instant with a great hand resting on the shoulder of his friend; but Red Hawk, looking him calmly in the eye, told him to join the rest.

So, in a moment, he was left alone. With his brow in his hand, he sat cross-legged beside the White Horse. There was no need for pondering. With the white race he had no place; and from the Indians he was cast out. Perhaps it remained for him to live like a lone wolf of the prairies, drifting here and there, alone. Even with the White Horse for a companion that desolate thought was more bitter than death to him. Death itself seemed the simplest way by which he could leave his troubles.

If that desire had been clear in him when he ventured into the house of Wind Walker, it was doubly strong at this moment. He could avoid the sin of self-destruction by going now into the house of a power far more terrible than Wind Walker himself. The thing loomed with a sudden certainty before him; he could see the picture of the great pillar which leaned at the gate of the Sacred Valley, and of himself moving small through the entrance and onto that ground where no Indian ever had stepped before him. It seemed to him that he could understand now that word which had been whispered in the air above him from the wings of the great night-owl those years ago. All of his wandering had been futile. Now he must go straight into the presence of the great spirit, Sweet Medicine.

He stripped himself, found some sweet grass, purified himself with the smoke, and dressed himself in some new leggings of deerskin. There was a new deerskin shirt; but when a man was to stand in the awful presence of Sweet Medicine it was fitting that the body should be naked above the waist.

He would have to be painted, or else the great spirit would not even know that he was a Cheyenne, perhaps. Therefore he mixed some red paint, and painted on his breast what seemed to him a speaking likeness of an owl, flying with outstretched wings. On his feet he drew a pair of beaded moccasins; he dressed his dark red hair with eagle feathers; and over his shoulders he drew a buffalo robe.

141

With a gesture he raised the White Horse to his feet.

So he stepped into the night with the shimmering figure of the great horse behind him, and went straight out from the camp.

Most of the Cheyennes had gone to sleep by this time, in spite of the great excitement caused by the arrival of the White Horse. But though the majority of the camp slept, there was still a sea of noise. Two or three sick babies were crying. Above all, the dogs maintained a steady uproar; there would not be a moment during the night when there was not at least one fight in progress, or one false alarm of "coyotes" to bring the pack hurrying out from the lodges into the open night.

One of those canine outpourings occurred at the very moment when Red Hawk left the camp. A great roaring wash of dogs swept out around him, yelled at the moonlit hills, and then receded again among the lodges.

Red Hawk, turning to watch them go back, saw a woman moving slowly after him. She came up without haste, until he could see the moon polishing the braids of her hair and the turn of her throat and above all the light of it was in her eyes. It was the Blue Bird.

When she was near, she waited for him to speak. A wind out of the valley whispered and tugged and fluttered about her, and he thought of the white girl in Witherell. She might be more delicately made, but she had not carried burdens, and therefore she did not stand as straight as the Blue Bird. And what could the white girl do except sing and turn the pages of a book?

But the hands of the Cheyenne woman were strong enough to grasp the heart of a man. Yes, and to fight for it, once held! He said to her:

"Blue Bird, it is a lucky thing that you have met me here."

142

"It is not luck. I have followed you," said the girl.

"Have you?" said he. "Well, I could give my message to no one else, but I can trust you. Stand here, where I can see you with the moon on your face. *Ah-hai! Ah-hai!*" he added, softly. "You have grown beautiful! I wish that I had sun—or even firelight—to see you by, so that I could find all the color. You had a golden face, and I can remember the color and the blue-black in your hair and eyes. Stand a little closer. Now turn your head to the right—so! You have grown beautiful because you are a little sad. Why are you sad, Blue Bird? Are there no young men among the Cheyennes?"

She looked straight back at him for a moment, until it was difficult for him to stare into her eyes. He watched her breathing, that made a ripple of light run down the two long braids of her hair falling forward over her shoulders.

"You have found a white girl," said Blue Bird. "That is why you talk to me like an old man to a child."

"I have found a white girl," he admitted. "But she goes to the lodge of another man."

He saw her hands gripping hard together, so that when he looked up into her face he expected to see some strong emotion. But she was as calm as an image that falls by moonlight into still water.

"You are leaving us again?" said the girl.

"I am walking out in the night for a time," said he.

"You are leaving us," said she. "You have made up your mind to do some great thing."

"Why do you say that?" he asked her.

"The war chief and the medicine man turn their backs on you. That you have brought in the White Horse is not enough to please them. Therefore you are going out to throw yourself away."

"How?"

143

"You will find a Pawnee camp and ride through it without a weapon, to count one grand victorious coup before you die."

He smiled. Compared with the dreadful thing that lay before him, what was a Pawnee camp filled with wolfish fighters?

"There is another way to die," said he. "Tell your father and Standing Bull and my father. I am going to the Sacred Valley.

"The white people laugh at me, and the chiefs of the Cheyennes turn their backs on me," he went on. "I am going into the house of Sweet Medicine to die."

"Wait for me to speak," she said, whispering. "I am going to say something."

He waited. The wind that pressed against her seemed to sway her a little from side to side, as a warrior is sometimes swayed when a spirit is working strongly in his throat, about to break forth into a great utterance.

But all she said was, at last:

"Farewell—Red Hawk!"

"To my father say this—" he began.

Then he saw that she was turning away from him, with her hands crossed on her breast. She went slowly back toward the moon-whitened lodges of the Cheyennes.

Something made him stare after her until she was lost among the shining tepees.

CHAPTER 24

WHEN Red Hawk rode the stallion up the ravine toward the Sacred Valley, it seemed to him that the walls of the gorge were ten times as deep as when he had come here with his foster father. He told himself that it was not death itself that he feared; what he dreaded was the moment when destruction approached, for there is agony of mind greater than any of the body. His thoughts were those of delirium.

He had expected that it would be full daylight when he reached the mouth of the valley; but in this calculation he had overlooked the speed of the White Horse, which rapidly unrolled the remembered silhouettes of the hills and brought him in the first of the dawn to the entrance of the valley.

He had made up his mind before. Perhaps it was more fitting that he should walk meekly, with bowed head, through the enormous gate; but since destruction was so near at hand, he had determined to ride in to meet it on the back of the White Horse.

Mounted, therefore, he made a short prayer holding out his hands: "Sweet Medicine, since you made the feathered wing of an owl speak to me in your name, I have been your man. But I am tired of traveling in sorrow, and so I have come back to look into your face. I am going to ride into your own valley. If I have done wrong, you will kill me quickly; but if you have pity on me, then you will let me go back to the world, and you will show me happiness among men."

When he had finished, he took the robe from around his shoulders, so that on his own bare breast Sweet Medicine might see the painted symbol of the owl. After that, Red Hawk rode straight forward to meet his destiny.

He was glad that there was a morning mist in the air, for its obscure rollings would hide whatever death ran upon him until just before its hand was at his throat. He threw open his arms and put back his head to receive the fatal stroke, as the White Horse carried him straight into the valley.

It seemed that something like a shadow crossed his mind. But now he saw before him only the green billowing of trees, on either side of the water that shunted down the slant, held quiet by its speed and the smoothness of its bed.

It was a forest which thronged all the throat of the valley, so that in a moment he was passing through a second night, dim and gray. The branches were polished with wet and blackness; they interlaced their fingers to continue overhead a billowing gloom.

The silence of the flowing river, which made only hushed sounds, was proof that Sweet Medicine wished the magic voice of his distant waterfall to be heard from afar. That noise was a chanting and a shouting and a trampling still far away when Red Hawk left the trees and came suddenly out into such a prospect as he had never seen before.

The morning mist had almost dispersed. Only walking wraiths moved from hillock to hillock, and flowings of translucent silver poured over the low places. The wet grass took the rosy sheen of the dawn like a dim lake; and here and there, and again in the distance, rose open groves of enormous trees that seemed to be standing in water.

Something moved out of the mist that still clung about the trunks of a grove of trees. Then one after another he

146

saw buffaloes stepping behind a lordly bull. By twenties and twenties they moved. They drew near; they paused; and all at once turned their shaggy eyes to behold him, without fear.

At that, Red Hawk's strength slid like water out of his heart, and he dropped from the White Horse to the ground. In the wet grass he lay face down and groaned with terror. Why should the buffalo fear him, when they were accustomed to the comings and goings of Sweet Medicine? He had entered a world of magic. The very taste of the air was different, and even the grass was not cold, but wet and warm against his flesh.

When he ventured to lift his head again, he saw that the monsters had vanished. The White Horse stood close by with lifted head, listening, listening.

He stood up, and the stallion crowded close to him. He made himself bold, and plucked up a handful of grass and offered it to the lips of the White Horse. But the stallion shook his head in a human gesture of refusal, and there was wonder in his eyes. At least, the wounding of the turf brought no instant punishment on Red Hawk's impious head and hand.

He walked on, the stallion ever pressing close behind him. They passed over a small rise, and in the hollow beyond, a whole herd of antelope stood frozen in attention. He waited for them to scatter before him like leaves on a wind of fear, but with bewildered eyes he saw them begin to graze again.

He walked straight down among them. None of them seemed to avoid him; though in their grazing they happened, as it were, to drift away from the line which he followed, so that a clear path was left before him. To right and left, he could have touched them. He saw their little black hoofs shining in the wet of the grass.

"Why should they be afraid?" said Red Hawk to his soul. "Arrows and bullets would turn aside from them. Sweet Medicine has breathed upon them, and steel edges cannot slay them."

He was walking through wild flowers. Wherever his eyes fell, beauty looked back at him; for this was the abode of a god, and where the feet of a god have rested—where even his eye has fallen—there is, of course, an enduring loveliness.

Only in one direction he dared not look, and that was toward the sound of the waterfall which called from the head of the valley. That was the visible semblance of the god; the eternal voice of Sweet Medicine. Strange to say, the realization of that fact was not overwhelming now. He drew nearer, moved by the side of the running water, letting it lead him toward its source. Sometimes his image wavered for an instant in a stillness of the shoal water at the side of the river; but usually there was nothing save froth and whirling.

Then a cool showering of spray wafted toward him. He looked up. Far above, the stream leaped out from the brow of the rock, pouring in the center like shuddering blue glass that whitened at the edges more and more, until the stream became a downpour of snowy spray. Some of that smoke was always blowing to the side. The morning color bloomed in it now.

Regathering, the water went swirling and twisting, clinging close to the rock all the way to the bottom of the cliff. Far above the voice of the waterfall sang, there was comparative silence. Once more a miracle of Sweet Medicine. For here was his living presence—his voice.

Something sliding in the air above him made Red Hawk turn his head and then fall on his knees, staring helplessly.

For there was the great night-owl, sliding overhead on easy wings!

CHAPTER 25

ONE instant, surely, he saw the sacred bird, there against the flaming sky; the great round head, the glint of the beak, the cruel talons tucked up in the soft down of the body feathers, with a red-stained something clutched in one foot. The next moment the thing was gone.

What is seen by the eye, the next instant will be felt by the flesh. Sweet Medicine had appeared; and now the stroke would fall. Red Hawk, very sick and small of heart, waited.

He searched the sky against which the owl had showed; but the bird did not again appear. He searched the upper face of the cliff, and there, not far from the verge of the cataract, he saw the mouth of a small cave. Fear made him dizzy when he looked on it, for he understood instantly what it must be. It was at that very place that Sweet Medicine had opened the heart of the mountain, and within that cave he had confronted the magicians and taken from them the holy arrows of the Cheyennes! Therefore he, Red Hawk, must mount to that perilous place.

This was the way death would come to him; this was the terrible agony of mind that he must endure before the final stroke. He must climb, with laboring feet, between earth and heaven, until at last he entered the black mouth of the cave. Then death—in the form of a monstrous owl, perhaps —would leap upon him and tear out his life with beak and talons.

He turned, and saw that the White Horse was shrinking back from him. For the first time since the stallion had come to his hand, it moved away from its master. Then, in a sudden panic the White Horse had fled away, sweeping along faster and faster.

Red Hawk looked after the fugitive with a melancholy eye. Even all the speed of that swiftest of horses would be of no avail, now that the wrath of Sweet Medicine hung overhead. The White Horse was gone. He would perish as a sacrifice unseen by his master; and for that Red Hawk was glad.

He began to climb. The way up the rock was not very hard. Sometimes, as he followed the windings of the easiest route, it seemed to him that his feet were falling on the time-obscured traces of steps that had been cut into the stone, ages ago. But this, he felt, must be an illusion.

The mist from the waterfall drenched a portion of the way, but his feet did not slip. Now that he was approaching the last moment of his life, they bore him steadfastly and strongly onwards.

At last, from a giddy height, he looked down and back. The whole valley lay spread before him. In another stride the bright sun would rise upon the day, and to some men would bring happiness.

He turned and faced the cave. The lower lip of that rocky mouth protruded to take him in. He stood on the narrow ledge for an instant, fighting the terror that made his knees weaken. In fact, the orifice of the cave was high enough to permit him to enter erect. He told himself that he must stride into the presence of Sweet Medicine like a man glad of his fate.

So, with an upward head, with a slow and dragging step, he forced himself into the teeth of darkness.

Only for a stride or two did the outer daylight follow

him, then all was swimming blackness. He could not tell whether he had taken three steps or thirty when he heard a rustling, as of feathers. A sound of many whispers rushed toward him. Eyes of burning gold shone at him, sped through his very brain, and he fell forward with a great cry.

Afterwards, he thought a hand of ice was on his forehead. He wakened to find that it was the cold of the rock. As he had lain before the house of Wind Walker, so he lay now, cold and shuddering. But death for the second time had refused to destroy him with its hand. This day it had not so much as broken his skin.

Fumbling to his feet, his hand touched a wooden stick, which he picked up as he rose. And now, turning, he saw the dull gleam of daylight to lead him from the gloom.

When he came to the lip of the cave, he was still too dizzy to stand upright, fearlessly. But sitting on his heels, he remembered what the truth must be. Between two things Sweet Medicine must make his choice; either to take at once the wretched life of his believer, or else give to that man happiness!

But was there any happiness? Was there happiness anywhere?

Aye, it was there at Red Hawk's feet, in the green of the valley and in the sun-bright running of the river. The light that poured on the flat-topped mountains beyond the valley was happiness, too. And happiness was in the trumpet-tongued voice that now rang from the floor of the ravine, where the stallion ran back and forth, already darkened by a sweat of anxious fear, and neighing above the uproar of the waterfall.

Happiness? The surety of it streamed through Red Hawk's soul like the brilliance of the day. If for him happiness meant the white girl in the far-off village, Sweet

151

Medicine would give her to him. If she were bound to marry another man—well, death is a solvent that burns away all bonds at a touch!

He began to laugh with such exaltation that he flourished his arms above his head. It was a gesture that made him consider for the first time the stick that was grasped in his hand. It was half an arrow, with the head still adhering to the broken stick!

The breath went out of Red Hawk as though he had been plunged into cold water. Only by degrees his eyes, dim with staring, made out the features of the time-rotted wood, and the flint point.

Certainty came flooding over the staggered brain of Red Hawk, and he took the precious thing in both hands. He cherished it against the warmth of his breast. For what could it be but one of those sacred arrows which long ago the magicians of the mountains had given to Sweet Medicine?

Happiness? The sky was cloven before him. Let the most hard-minded among the Cheyennes dare to doubt that he had walked into the presence of the god, when he returned, carrying in his hand this proof.

He was hungry, suddenly, for the smoke which might be breathed forth in ceremonial praise of Sweet Medicine.

He stood up. The steep face of the rock seemed to him of no more danger than if he had worn wings at his shoulders to keep him from a fall. Laughing he went down the slippery descent, leaped over the rill of water that ran across the foot of it.

He would not ride, at once. Riding would carry him too quickly out of the Sacred Valley, which was now his valley, for was he not free of it?

Into every corner of the valley he wandered, and found everywhere that same enchanting combination of great

152

trees and open meadows. One who cared to dwell here would never need to ask a thing from the hand of the outer world. In the brush he saw numbers of mountain grouse. A moment later, he discovered a herd of splendid elk.

He told himself that this was the place where he would pitch his lodge or build his house, on side of the lake overlooking the big sweep of the outer valley.

A little creek above the lake was a bright and singing beauty that could not go straight for a moment, but danced from side to side in the brilliance of the sun. It seemed to him that the very pebbles of the creek shone with a light of their own—a rich and metallic yellow.

He leaned and scooped up a handful of the little stones, and of the bright sand. He was amazed to find that it weighted his hand far more than ever rocks could do.

The White Horse came and nibbled curiously at him, then tossed his head and turned away in disdain. But Red Hawk began suddenly to shout, for he knew that he held in his hands the god of the white men—Gold!

CHAPTER 26

RED HAWK got his buffalo robe and tied into a corner of it the product of half a day of scraping in the riffles and washing in the brightest sand of the creek. When he had finished, he had twenty pounds of gold, some fine as dust, some in heavy nuggets.

After that, as he followed down the course of the stream to the point where it joined the main river, his eyes searched the sand and gravel everywhere. And everywhere he saw the winking yellow eyes of the treasure. Still he laughed! For was it not fitting that the Indian god should live on the heights, while the god of the white man lay in the mud of the valley below him?

He went on down the valley in the middle of the afternoon. Two of the buffalo bulls were fighting. Beating the ground, they slashed the turf with their hoofs. They were still bumping their heads together as he passed on into the lower ravine, and so through the quiet filled by the hushing sound of the stream until he was near the gates of the valley.

Here he paused for a moment, because his blood turned cold as he recognized out of the distance the monotonous death chant of the Cheyennes. Was it a song sent by Sweet Medicine to warn him from the entrance? Was he to be imprisoned here all the rest of his days?

He stepped out beside the leaning pillar and saw, beyond him, at the edge of the swift water, a full fifty of the warriors of the tribe. They were singing together, and before them all old Spotted Antelope kneeled on the ground in nothing but a breechclout. He was wailing to the god, the song shaking his fat paunch as he raised his time-dwindled arms to the sky. Close behind him was the second group of mourners, composed of Standing Bull and Lazy Wolf. It was not strange that these three should have come—but behind them in a wide semicircle were other braves, and among them no less a magnificence than Running Elk, the great medicine man!

They saw Red Hawk at the same time, as he came out with the White Horse behind him; and they broke into a shout that was the sweetest music he ever had listened to in his life. Then they came pouring about him.

A spirit came on Red Hawk. He held up the broken arrow before their eyes and was silent. All the way back to

154

the camp he would not speak, neither to the smiling face of Standing Bull nor to the exulting eyes of old Spotted Antelope, nor to Lazy Wolf, who kept bumping his heels against the side of his mule.

On the way, in spite of his own silence, he learned why the warriors had come. The Blue Bird had repeated the story of how Red Hawk had left the camp to find the face of Sweet Medicine, whereupon it was suddenly revealed to Running Elk that perhaps the heart of the great spirit would be turned from the tribe because of the sad prayers of Red Hawk. Therefore, in the middle of the night he had called on chosen warriors. Only Dull Hatchet had refused to come; the rest had been singing the lament to pacify Sweet Medicine.

It was deep night before they reached the camp. The scouts who met them turned back with whoopings that raised the whole village; and Red Hawk, still silent, led the way not to the lodge of his father, but to that central opening among the tepees where the ceremonial fuel was piled high to await a happening sufficient for celebration.

Dull murmurs and the movement of feet told him that the circle was now ringed about by many people. In the distance, children cried out in sharp voices, which were hushed suddenly as they drew nearer.

In the meantime, Red Hawk took from Standing Bull flint and steel. Onto a quantity of dry timber he shed the shower of sparks until the flame caught. Now the fire put up a slender waving finger. He pushed the flaming little pile against the great heap, and watched the fire run up the side of the mound until the whole mass was a roaring blaze. Now, as he turned, he saw the firelight over the faces of the throng.

He stretched his hand into the sky. He began to walk up and down, holding the broken arrow in his hand. Now and

155

then he leaped into the air, and again strode on. Some one began to rumble a drum, softly. A flute screamed out. In the pauses of that music he began his chant.

At the entrance flap of the great lodge that faced south onto the circle, he saw Dull Hatchet standing, gathered into the darkness of a buffalo robe.

"Who stood in the medicine lodge at the time of the initiation?" cried Red Hawk. "Who stood in the medicine lodge and heard a voice saying: 'Turn from the blood! Turn from the blood! Go out from this place!' Who stood in the medicine lodge?"

The whole throng gathered up the name and sent it booming, strong with the long suspense of speech, "Red Hawk!"

"It was the voice of Sweet Medicine that spoke," said Red Hawk. "Whose spirit did he melt? Whose heart did he soften? Whose feet did he lead from the lodge?"

"Red Hawk!" cried that deep voice of men, that tingling voice of the women and children.

"I see a man walking on the plains," he chanted. "He follows the trail of the White Horse, from winter to summer. For Sweet Medicine leads him on, through snow and over burning ground; starving, thirsting. Now I see him walking away from the mountains, and the White Horse follows him. The White Horse comes to his hand. What man is he?"

"Red Hawk!" shouted the crowd.

The small boys had worked through to the front of the circle by this time; and as the pauses came and the drums thundered and the people cried out, the little naked boys shouted the response with a voice as shrill as the crowing of roosters.

"He has come to his people again," he chanted. "I see him among the famous Cheyennes, but the hearts of the

156

leaders are blackened; they turn from him. What man is he?"

"Red Hawk!" came that yelling answer.

The dark form of Dull Hatchet moved a little from in front of his lodge. Old Running Elk, hideous in a buffalo mask, came prancing out from the line and began a dance, moving his head and body up and down like a turkey gobbler that curtsies to his own pride, the while shaking long rattles made of bones.

The heart of Red Hawk swelled at this sight, for he saw that the chief medicine man of the tribe was giving his presence and his credit to the chant. Running Elk was paying homage.

"At the door of the Sacred Valley—at the leaning pillar —at the entrance to the house of the god—in the path of danger—by the swift, whispering water—what man do I see?" he cried.

"Red Hawk!" they thundered back at him.

"The air is white as milk. It is like the breathing of buffaloes in winter. The trees are as monsters under water; they are as spirits. For this is the floor of the lodge of Sweet Medicine. This is the Sacred Valley that I see, and a man goes riding through it on a white horse.

"The mist clears. About the man move the sacred buffalo, fearless. The little fawns stretch out their bright, wet muzzles to his hand. They belong to Sweet Medicine, and they are not afraid. What man is he?"

"Red Hawk!" shouted a greater chorus than ever.

In the distance, on the verge of the circle, Red Hawk saw the face of the Blue Bird. For one instant it was like a jewel held in the dark hand of the night. Beyond her, he saw the great buffalo robe slip away from the naked shoulders of Dull Hatchet.

"The magic waters fall from the cliff. They speak from

157

the sky. Their throat is the throat of Sweet Medicine. I see the face of a man wet with their spray. I see him look up, and over his head flies the night-owl, huger than ever an owl was seen before. The bird has vanished. It is no longer in the sky. Ay, for there is a hole in the rock. And I see the man walk up the face of the cliff. His feet cling like the feet of a mountain goat to the ledges, and he stands at the black mouth of the cave. What man is he?"

"Red Hawk!" bellowed the throng.

Standing out above the rest, towering even above those tall warriors who encircled the fire, he saw Dull Hatchet wading through the throng. Slowly he came, stretching out an arm before him to make his way.

"I see a man enter the cave of blackness. It is the heart of the mountain where Sweet Medicine found the magicians. It is the dreadful chamber where he found the magic arrows, and which gave fortune to the Cheyennes. It is filled with darkness, but the man walks on. What man is he?"

"Red Hawk! Red Hawk!" they roared.

He began to be frenzied, shouting out as the thundering of the drums died away again:

"Out of the blackness of the cave I see a monster coming. Swifter than the feet of men he is coming. His eyes are two golden moons that fly toward the man. Something is thrust into his hand. He hears a voice that whispers: 'Peace!' He hears a noise of wings. He falls into a darkness of the mind.

"He rises again at last. He comes out to the day. He looks down at his body and sees that it is alive. On his breast the red owl is painted. In his hand there is a token, for him and for all the Cheyennes. It is a magic arrow. It is an arrow out of the old time. It is a medicine arrow to bring happiness to the Cheyennes. And he lifts the arrow. He brings it to his people. He tells them the truth with a single tongue. He holds the arrow before their eyes. What man is he?"

But the whole circle of the listeners began to crumble as they heard the climax of the adventure. Now there arose a veritable shrieking that sent his own name into his ears in roaring waves.

He saw Spotted Antelope staggering towards him, drunk with joy. He saw Standing Bull leaping like a frantic colt. But most of all the amazed face and the staring eyes of Dull Hatchet, as the war chief strode towards him, still brushing aside the lesser people with his scarred and massive arms. So Red Hawk knew that he had at last come home, indeed, to the heart of his tribe.

CHAPTER 27

THE progressive spirit and the business aggressiveness of Jeremy Bailey and his brother Joe were building Witherell into a trading post that promised to be a great success. Joe Bailey had gone out onto the plains and induced the chiefs of the Pawnees to bring in a camp of several hundred lodges, and they now whitened the pass leading down to the town.

Jeremy Bailey, on the other hand, had brought down the creek to the town several big scows loaded down with articles for the Indian trade. Every brave among those Pawnees had his share of skins and furs and buffalo robes which he was prepared to trade for knives, guns, ammunition, colored calico, the blankets which were lighter than buffalo robes could ever be, bright beads, sugar, coffee, tea, iron pots, and the sail canvas which more and more was coming to be used in place of the heavy lodges made of skins.

All of these essentials in the trade were piled along the counters behind the various booths of the Bailey store. There had been three days of entertaining the chiefs and distributing presents to those greedy fellows. Now for two days the market had been opened, and the price had been agreed on at half a pint of sugar for a buffalo robe in good condition, with other things going in about the same proportion. If a white man could not make a profit of several thousand per cent, it was hardly considered worth while to be in the Indian trade.

Such happiness came over Jeremy Bailey's mind that he looked across the room, through the air which was dust-clouded from the handling of the robes, and even smiled when his glance rested on the face of his brother. They did not love one another; they never had. But today Jeremy could forgive the world that had harnessed him to a twin. They were necessary to one another; Joe because he was the tactful one who brought in new business, and Jeremy because he had the calculating eye and mind that drives good bargains.

The trading was going on at a fine rate when a little murmur ran among the Pawnees; and in one instant every booth under the big, sprawling awning was deserted. What the whisper had been Jeremy could not tell, but instantly he was ready for a fight. If another trader had showed up to tempt away the Pawnees, there was blood in the eye of Jeremy.

He shrugged his shoulders and strode out of the trading store in time to see a rider come around the next corner and into the central square of the town. He was mounted on a white horse, and behind him streamed out a fan-shaped tail of small boys, all yelling and whooping. The rider himself sat in the usual Indian saddle, his feet very high, his back humped forward a good deal, his head bobbing up and down a little with every step of the horse. However, Jeremy Bailey was accustomed to the sight of Indian braves on ponies.

It was the horse itself that caught the eye of Jeremy, and his face flushed until the scar on it stood out like white paint. Then, as he saw the glint of the sun on the dark red hair of the man, he realized that he knew all about him. That was the famous stallion, and the rider was the white Cheyenne called Red Hawk.

Jeremy Bailey sighed with relief. The grimness went out of his eye, but the greed remained in it as he stared at the horse. That horse would be the extra touch, the little garnishing, which would smooth his way with Maisry Lester. If he were to appear astride the White Horse he was sure that the sight would move something in the heart of the girl. It would even stir her father, whose cold, suspicious eyes seemed always to be hunting for the truth, and coming near to the fact that his daughter was marrying in order to provide for her parents.

Jeremy thought of these things, and then permitted himself to admire the way this white Cheyenne rode heedlessly through a crowd of the roach-headed Pawnees, the ancient enemies of his tribe. To be sure, for the moment they were too overcome with astonishment and pleasure at the sight of the horse to be capable of action. Nevertheless, it seemed to the trader that Red Hawk was most perilously placed.

Yet the white Indian rode straight on, never turning eye to right or left, until he dismounted suddenly before Jeremy. The White Horse began to rub his head against the shoulder of his master, keeping a wary eye on the Indians,

161

who stole around them.

"You are Jeremy Bailey," said the newcomer. "My name is Red Hawk, and I have come to make a trade with you."

Jeremy Bailey considered that sun-darkened face and the deep blue stain of the eyes in it. He had the look of one who had suffered; of one who has escaped from a long illness and achieved out of it some sort of spiritual happiness. For a man who had built up such a name, he was small; not much above middle height, and rather slenderly made. Bulk of thews and sinews always seemed a necessity to big Jeremy Bailey.

"You've got no robes with you that I can see," said Jeremy. "But if you want to trade in the horse, we might talk business."

"Trade in the horse?" asked the white Cheyenne.

He turned his head and smiled at the great stallion. He put out his hand and twisted his fingers into the forelock of the big horse while he answered, absently:

"I have something else to trade with you."

He took a pouch that was slung from his shoulder, opened the mouth of it, and took out something which Bailey could not see until the cold, small weight of it was laid in his hand. Then he saw the sheen of gold, and his fingers furled instantly over the nugget.

"In the name of God!" said Jeremy.

"True," said the white Cheyenne, calmly. "I have brought you your god. There is a great deal more of him. This bag is full, and that is why I want to trade."

"More of him! You know a place where you can get more of this?" asked Bailey.

"I know a place where the sands of a creek are yellow with it," said Red Hawk. "But you could not go there. No white man; no red man can go there. None except Red Hawk."

162

"Why not?" asked Bailey.

"Because there is bad medicine there for other men."

"Medicine be damned! Where—"

He checked himself and swallowed. He looked down at the ground and hoped that the lust had not burned too brightly in his eyes.

"Come with me!" said Jeremy Bailey. "We'll go inside."

"Outside," answered Red Hawk. "The horse must stay with me. If we went inside, he would beat down the wall to come after me."

So Bailey took him around to the rear of the store, where no wind stirred and where the heat brought out the sweat instantly, covering the face with ten thousand small, shining beads.

"Is that bag full of the stuff?" Jeremy Bailey demanded sharply.

"Yes."

"How long did it take you to wash it out?"

"Most of it I picked out of the riffles on the face of the rock," said Red Hawk. "The rest I washed out of the gravel with my hands. It took me half a day."

Jeremy Bailey lifted the bag. This man, with his ignorant hands, had taken out of the ground five or six thousand dollars in half a day!

At last Jeremy Bailey looked up. His voice came out with a surprising roundness and evenness.

"And what do you want me to give you for this? How much calico and how many knives do you want?" asked Jeremy.

"Calico and knives?" repeated Red Hawk contemptuously. "I bring you the body of your god. I give it into your hands. And you want to trade me knives and dyed cloth!"

Bailey flushed. "Well, then?" he asked.

"I want your woman," said Red Hawk simply.

Bailey stared at him, shaking his head without comprehension.

"The woman who is to be your squaw in a little time," Red Hawk continued. "I will give you the body of your god for your woman."

"You damned—" began Jeremy Bailey.

Then it occurred to him that this was no time to be righteously indignant, when he was standing with his hand on the very Wishing Gate itself.

"Well," said he, "the girl I'm to marry is what you mean? Maisry Lester?"

"I give you all the gold that is in this sack," answered Red Hawk.

Bailey shook his head. "Not for this. But if you'll take me to the place where the gold is—that's another matter, Red Hawk. We might arrange something then. We could do business together there, my friend!"

"Very well," answered Red Hawk, smiling. "I knew that you would be willing. Let us go to the woman, at once; then you can tell her that I am buying her away from you."

"Hold on!" said the trader. "I can't give her away, perhaps. I can't deliver her to you, I don't suppose. I don't know. I'll have to have a chance to think over what can be arranged. Don't hurry me, Red Hawk. Let me think. I'll satisfy you, one way or another. But I can't simply walk up to her and tell her that she's been traded to another man."

"Can you not tell her that you take your hands from her and make her free?"

"Yes," said Bailey. "Of course I could do that. But what—"

"That is all I ask," said Red Hawk. "Come—and we'll go quickly to her."

CHAPTER 28

IN every respect, Jeremy Bailey was a practical man, but now he hesitated for a moment with his head bowed, his face reddening, his glance going up under his brows at Red Hawk. This was the moment when his twin brother, Joe Bailey, stepped around the corner of the building and said, smiling:

"Why not, Jerry? A woman can't say anything as heavy as gold."

Jeremy, staring at his brother, understood suddenly that his conversation with Red Hawk had been overheard. He began to walk towards Joe, taking short steps.

"What's the good of trying to murder me, Jerry?" asked Joe calmly. "You'd be hanged before you had a chance to collect the loot and enjoy it. Don't be a fool! I'm in on this deal, but I'll be worth my salt before the finish. You'll find that out. I've always been worth my salt to you."

"So you're declaring yourself in on this, are you?" demanded Jeremy. "I pay blood for a chance at the gold mine; and you pay nothing but ten minutes of your damned time spying on me. And you declare yourself in on it!"

"Take it easy," advised Joe. "Suppose I tell the other men in town that Red Hawk has brought in a sack of gold that he washed out, with his own hands in a half day. Well, after that what chance will you have to get away and find the mine? You'd be watched night and day. There'd never be a minute when the people here in Witherell wouldn't have their horses saddled and ready for the start. Think it over, Jeremy. You'll need a partner, anyway. This isn't the matter of a small haul. There's millions in this, maybe!"

"Shut up, you fool!" exclaimed Jeremy, looking askance at Red Hawk.

But the latter merely said quietly: "All the sands of the creek are shining with your god. You can pick him by the mule load—"

A frantic signal for silence ended this speech.

"Take him over and have a chat with Maisry," Joe went on. "She'll understand. She's not a fool. She knows that business is business." And he began to laugh, nodding his head at his brother.

Jeremy Bailey cursed, softly, profoundly. At last he snapped his fingers and remarked:

"It has to be done, I suppose. Look here, Red Hawk, what the devil fixes your eyes on that girl? Even if I back out of the picture, you probably can't have her. She's more likely to take up with a fellow of her own kind; some one raised in her own way, I mean. You can pick up a hundred good squaws. I'll load down ten horses for you with stuff out of the store, and with any one load of that, you'll be able to buy for yourself the prettiest girl among the Cheyennes. Doesn't that sound good to you?"

Red Hawk listened gravely until the speech was finished. Then he placed his hand on the neck of the stallion.

"For two years," he said, "I hunted the White Horse to please her. Why do you talk to me about blankets and knives and ammunition and sugar, when I am thinking of the girl herself?"

"You see?" said Joe to his brother. "And what's the difference? You can blush five minutes, and be rich the rest of your life!"

"May you rot in hell!" said Jeremy softly, and waving to

166

Red Hawk to follow him, he walked off at a brisk pace while Joe remained behind, rubbing his knuckles across his chin.

After an instant, however, Joe decided to join the others, and set off after them with long strides.

They went across the back fences, the brothers slipping between the bars and Red Hawk vaulting the barriers with the White Horse. So they came to the rear of Lester's house, and saw his daughter irrigating a vegetable patch.

The girl looked toward them silently; at Red Hawk first, and finally at Jeremy Bailey. Jeremy said:

"Maisry, every man has his price. Red Hawk has found mine. If I back down and keep away from you, he'll give me a fortune. Just how he'll give it I can't tell you. But the price is too high for me. You never gave a rap about me, and so now I'm pulling out."

He stopped. Red Hawk could hear his loud breathing.

The girl had on old leather gloves that had once belonged to her father, and which were now torn and blackened by the garden work. She took off one of those gloves so that with her bare fingers she could arrange her hair, pushing a loose, bright strand into the shimmering mass.

"Why, Jeremy," she said placidly, "the people who make bargains ought always to be free to break them, I suppose. It's quite all right."

"About your father," said Jeremy, huskily. "I want to say that I still intend to help you to—"

She had not even lifted her hand, but her quiet eyes stopped him, and Red Hawk was filled with wonder.

"Go and saddle your horses," Red Hawk said to Jeremy. "When you come past the front of the house, I shall be ready."

"I wanted to say," said Jeremy to the girl, his face bright with sweat, "that if—"

"Come along, Jeremy!" commanded his brother. "Don't be making a fool of yourself. It's over, now. Come along with me!"

He took Jeremy's arm in his hand and pulled him away, and Jeremy's face was red and polished as if it had been mahogany.

Red Hawk's heart drank of joy in much the same way that the thirsty soil drank up the water which the girl gave to it.

He was smiling as he looked up at the girl; then his smile went out. She was not stern; rather, infinitely quiet. Time went on like a sailing bird; time, which cannot pause except at the end of life, seemed to have halted utterly for her.

Out of that moment of quiet she said to him, "So you have bought me, Red Hawk?"

"How can I buy you?" he asked her. "I can tie a hundred horses to the poles in front of your father's lodge; but if you will not have me, and if he will not give you to me, still you are not mine. However, I have showed Jeremy Bailey the body of his god, and I am going to take him where he can get the rest of it. What I showed to him I can also give to you. If your god is strong, perhaps, there is enough of him here in this bag to take care of your father and mother. If not, perhaps I can bring more."

Unslinging the bag from his shoulder, he poured the contents suddenly on the ground before her feet. Some of the nuggets jumped away and sank out of sight in the soft, liquid mud of the vegetable patch. Others lay half buried, half dimmed by the dust.

As he straightened he was surprised to see that she was not looking at the gold, but into his face; she was smiling as women smile at a child.

"My father is a proud man," said the girl. "What do you

168

think he will say when I show him this and say it is offered for me?"

"He will say," said Red Hawk, instantly, "that first I brought the White Horse and then I brought gold, and that after that there is something greater, which is a need that I have of you. For the knife that fits the hand is not thrown away, even when it is old and almost worn away by grinding. That is how you fit into my mind. I could never buy you. I could not buy the White Horse, either; but each of us belongs to the other, and cannot be put out of mind."

To this she made an answer that seemed to him evasive, though she no longer smiled at him. She began to move her eyes by pauses over his face.

"You were sick when you were last in Witherell," she said. "Your face was all bones and sorrow, but now you are happier. You look younger, and you look able to laugh. Why is that? Is there something in the wild story that has drifted into the town about the white Cheyenne who went to the Sacred Valley and saw Sweet Medicine, and brought back a sacred arrow to his tribe?"

She was smiling again, but there was a poison of whimsical mockery in the smile.

Very troubled, he said, "That is true."

"True?" she exclaimed. "True that you saw Sweet Medicine—and that he gave you a sacred arrow with his own hand? I'd like to hear about it."

In that moment she had withdrawn to a great distance from him. He put out his hand, but saw that no physical effort could draw her back to him. He said simply:

"Yes, it is true. I alone, with the White Horse, entered the Sacred Valley. I went beyond the leaning pillar which no Indian has ever passed. And I came close up to the feet of the speaking waters. I looked up and saw the owl of

Sweet Medicine fly into a cave far up the rock. I climbed up the cliff and stood before the dark of the cave."

"Were you terribly afraid?" she asked him.

He sighed, answering, "If we are to know one another, we must have the whole truth. Yes, I was terribly afraid. I was so afraid that every breath I drew froze my heart. Only my feet carried me inside, and there in the darkness I saw the two golden eyes of Sweet Medicine. I fell on my face, and heard the rushing of his robes over my head, and a whisper that said, 'Peace!' When I stood up, I found that in my hand there was a broken arrow, very ancient. No man has seen an arrowhead chipped like the one I found in the cave of Sweet Medicine."

"Do you think it might not have been Sweet Medicine, but only an owl that you frightened out of its cave?" she asked him.

He smiled at her, for he could see that she was coming back to him swiftly; that she was drawing very near again.

"Let me tell you this," said Red Hawk. "Every tribe on the plains sees different spirits. The Pawnees see a Corn Mother. The Sioux see other Listeners under the ground and above. Perhaps the gods take many shapes, and if a white man had been able to see in that darkness of the cave he would have said that the rustling of the robe was only the wings of a bird beating the air and that the golden moons were the eyes of an owl. I cannot tell. To the Cheyennes, it was Sweet Medicine, and the great spirit will grant us good fortune because of the broken arrow. But what will you say to me, Maisry? I am not trying to buy words of you with the yellow god of the white man. What will you say to me?"

"First," she said, "take up the gold. It is yours. My father will not accept it, and neither may I."

"If it is not good for you, it is not good for me. Let it

170

sink in the mud therefore," said he.

She looked down from his face, suddenly, as though she were seeing the glimmering little pile of metal for the first time.

"Will you give me a little more time?" she said, anxiously. "If I were free, I would follow you this moment. Do you believe me?"

"Your lips have said it. Therefore, it is true," said Red Hawk. "I knew that this would be true, because the strength of Sweet Medicine came with me all the way across the plains. Therefore, I have been sure of happiness. I must go away now. From now until the moon is full and has worn away again to the first quarter, I shall be busy. At the end of that time I shall come again."

"What is it you wish to do in all that time?" she asked.

"I have promised to show Jeremy Bailey where the yellow body of the white man's god lies," he said, "and then I return."

CHAPTER 29

WHEN Red Hawk saw the Bailey brothers coming up the street a moment later and sent the White Horse vaulting over the fences to meet them, he halted them and the string of pack mules which had been prepared so quickly for the two traders. Then he rode down to the square and halted at each corner of it.

"Friends of Wind Walker, tell him that between the full of the moon and the half, Dull Hatchet and Standing Bull and Red Hawk shall hunt for him among the Witherell

171

Hills, between the peak with two summits and the white hill. Let him come, and bring two friends with strong hands, because three Cheyennes will be waiting for him."

Four times he called that speech, from the four corners of the square. Then he turned and smiled as he found the eyes of the many clinging to him, following him—and most of all huge Sam Calkins, who stood in front of his shop, all soot and shimmering sweat. For how could all of these people know that in fact there was little or no danger to the Cheyennes in the battle to come, since Sweet Medicine had given to the tribe freshly favoring good fortune?

Once they were started, the mules reached across the plains in long marches, for mules take short steps, but they are never tired. There were six of those mules, besides the riding horses of the Bailey brothers; and every one of the mules, they said, would be loaded with the yellow god before they turned back to the towns of men. They talked as though they could pack heaven on the backs of the six mules.

"We'll pack half a million!" said Jeremy to Joe.

Red Hawk, listening indifferently, said to them, "I am your guide and not your guard. You know that the Sacred Valley has been entered by only one man. I am that man. Are you not foolish, then, to go past the leaning pillar?"

They laughed at him.

"How will Sweet Medicine hit us, Red Hawk?" they asked him. "With thunder and lightning?"

They kept on laughing while he watched them with calm, incurious disgust, as though they were walking deaths.

Yet he went first, when they came to the leaning pillar at the entrance to the Sacred Valley, and they followed, with their rifles prepared, looking cautiously from side to

172

side. Blind fools who thought that they could see a god, as it seemed to Red Hawk.

He was amazed when, looking back, he saw that they had safely passed the pillar. He had been sure that they would die on the threshold of this holy place. However, who can determine the mind or predict the ways of the spirits?

These two men now hurried on with stony faces, as though fate already had entered them. They passed the thunder of the waterfall, speaking magic with deep tones, and in a short time they were entering the narrow upper ravine where the gold had been found.

The Sacred Valley seemed to have shrunk in size since Red Hawk had first come there. But what may not a god do in his own dwelling?

They were halfway up the stream when Joe Bailey screamed out an unintelligible word. With pain, but not with surprise, Red Hawk looked back, expecting to see that Sweet Medicine had already struck and that the man would be lying dead on the ground. Instead, he was on his knees, scooping sand and gravel up from the shallow bottom of the creek, and letting it drip out of his fingers. Showing his yellow-gilded palms to his brother, they laughed and shrieked. Then Joe hurled the first gold he had washed far away into the grass. He was mad, Red Hawk concluded. Sweet Medicine was touching the mind of the white men before he touched their bodies!

Jeremy was in the water, too, now. Then the pair of them were out and at one of the mule packs, tearing it apart and feverishly bringing out the shovels and wooden cradles for washing the gravel. They laid down buckskin sacks. Without pausing to remove more than that one pack, they worked on wildly all the rest of that day.

Truly it was wonderful to see how the stream turned

yellow and black; and when they trenched into the sod beside the stream, they washed out portions of the deeply underlying stratum of sand, and this was as rich as the creek bed itself.

For some time Red Hawk watched them. They were already soaked to the skin, and their eyes were like the eyes of hungry beasts. He felt that he could endure the sight of them no more.

He looked up to the blue peace of the sky, and saw a single white cloud floating and melting in it. Perhaps that was Sweet Medicine, watching and smiling at these fools who thought that they could invade his house without punishment. Let not the blow that involved the pair strike on the faithful heart of a white Cheyenne!

Finally he set about unpacking. When the mules had been hobbled to graze, he built an open fireplace of rocks, cementing them together with mixed mud and long grass. Then he put up the shelter tent made of thick sail cloth. He would remain with them that one night, if indeed Sweet Medicine held his hand so long.

Then he took a rifle and went out to hunt. He passed a group of black-tailed deer almost at once, but he could not murder creatures which looked at him without fear. Luck, in the late afternoon, gave him sight of a mountain sheep that stood on the verge of a cliff, facing the brightness in the west. He tumbled it to the valley floor with a bullet through the head, and took off as much of the best meat as he could carry.

That burden he brought back to the camp which he had pitched beneath the spread of a mighty tree, and found that the Bailey brothers had glutted their first hunger for gold and now lay with their backs against the trunk of a tree, smoking.

The sun was out of sight behind the western heights, but it was not yet down. All the upper sky was brilliant with the pure light as Red Hawk put down the fresh meat and called to the brothers:

"Here is something to put in hungry bellies. Make your coffee as you choose to make it, while I roast some of this on spits."

They said nothing in reply. They looked at one another in silence, as though each was too tired to fall to any sort of work, even for the sake of hunger. In the meantime, Red Hawk busied himself in the kindling of the fire, the cutting up of the meat in small gobbets that would fit on some long splinters of wood that he had prepared.

All at once he heard one of the brothers come up behind him, dragging a rope that made a whispering sound in the grass. He did not even look aside as he said:

"That noise is like a snake coming, friend!"

Something cut the air over his head with a whispering sound. The noose of the rope fell over his body and jerked tight. He was flung on his back, with his arms pinned against his sides and bound fast below the elbows. Above him appeared the scarred face of Jeremy Bailey.

"Easy, Joe, eh?" said he.

"It don't take a man to handle a blind fool like him," said Joe Bailey.

Red Hawk lay still and looked at the sky. His mind was clear. He felt the damp cool of the turf seeping through his deerskin shirt.

Joe Bailey stood by and kicked him heavily in the ribs. "What does Sweet Medicine say about this, you half wit?" he asked.

"Get that other rope and we'll tie him hard," said Jeremy.

"Why not bash him over the head now and have done with it?" asked Joe.

"Because I want to talk to him for a minute. I want to tell him a few things about his Sweet Medicine. Yeah, *sweet* medicine it's going to be for you, Red Hawk!"

Red Hawk made no effort to struggle. They had revolvers at their hips, and knives in their belts; and they could cut him to pieces before he moved twice. More than that, this was the very floor of the house of the god—his voice spoke yonder and seemed to fill the sky. Therefore it was plain that all things were in his hands and that nothing could happen here except of his will.

In the meantime, he was tied hand and foot. Jeremy Bailey took him by the hair of the head, with one hand, and dragged him until his shoulders were propped against the trunk of the tree. Then the two brothers filled pipes and sat down cross-legged before him. They blew the smoke toward his face.

He merely said, "Why do you want to kill me? People kill men they hate or men they're afraid of. Why do you hate me, or why do you fear me?"

"Tell him, Jeremy," said Joe. "I hate to talk to the damned Cheyenne! I'd rather take and smash in his head for him and have it finished. You tell him why, will you?"

"Did you think, you poor idiot," said Jeremy, smiling into the eyes of Red Hawk, "that we'd let you get away from here to sell the news about this placer strike to somebody else? Look yonder!" He pointed. "You see those two little snaky-looking buckskin sacks?" he demanded.

"I see them," said Red Hawk.

"There's about twenty-five pounds of dust in each of 'em," explained Jeremy. "We've washed around twelve thousand dollars' worth of gold—in a part of one day. Hell, we've taken out of the ground in one day more than we've worked for all the other years of our lives! And you think that we'd let you walk free out of here to tell other people?"

"I understand," said Red Hawk.

"Good!" said Jeremy. "Then you understand one reason why you've got to be shut up for good and all. There's other reasons of my own. I'll tell you the best of 'em. I didn't like the way Maisry looked at you the other day. It made me a little sick to see a white girl look like that at a damned Cheyenne!"

Joe got up and stretched himself. "We'd better get it over with," he said, and pulled out a revolver.

"Wait a minute!" said Jeremy. "I want to talk to the fool for another minute. I want to ask him how much faith he has in his damned red god, just now. What's Sweet Medicine going to do for you, Red Hawk? Eh? You're the brave boy who got the sacred arrow out of the sacred cave, in the sacred mountain of the sacred valley. Eh? And what's the god going to do for the sacred Red Hawk who managed all of these sacred things? You tell me, will you?"

"Yeah," sneered Joe. "How scared are you?"

Red Hawk looked up at the sky through the wide design which the branches spread against the color. It was not exactly fear that he felt, rather a holy awe. He said:

"I am not afraid. I am only excited. I am excited as people are when they have a bet on a horse race and the horses are standing ready at the start."

"And a damned long race you're gonna run, in a couple of seconds," commented Jeremy. "So you ain't scared? You're only excited, eh?"

"You have guns," said Red Hawk. "And with a touch of your fingers you may send me death. But Sweet Medicine

177

is swifter and stronger by far. That is why I am excited, because I wait to see how he will touch you before my eyes."

"Now tell me something," said Jeremy, taking out a revolver and resting the barrel of it across his knee. "Before I sink a slug in you and then go to roast the meat that you hunted for us, are you going to admit that Sweet Medicine is no god at all? Are you going to admit he's just a plain damned owl that you happened to run into?"

Red Hawk frowned with profound consideration. "I do not think so," he said. "Am I to understand the mind of a spirit? Perhaps he will let me die because I have allowed two white men to come into the Sacred Valley. That I cannot tell. Afterwards, he will strike you."

"Will he?" said Jeremy. "It kind of makes me mad, Joe, to hear the way the fool sticks to his story. It kind of makes me mad to think that's the way he'll be thinking when he passes out and turns cold. He won't have any horrors. He'll still feel that he's in the hand of his god. It sort of takes the satisfaction out of lifting his hair, doesn't it?"

"Yes—it does," admitted Joe, in a strained voice. "It does—sort of."

He had been standing rigid behind his brother, his head straining back, his lower jaw thrust out, his eyes staring down under their lids. With the last words he spoke, the revolver in his hand lifted. Leaning, he fired straight down into Jeremy's back.

Jeremy fell on his face and gripped the grass with both hands. Joe fired into him again.

It seemed almost as though the impact of the bullet had caused Jeremy to rebound from the soil, for as his body flopped clumsily over, Red Hawk saw the gleam of a gun in his hand, too.

178

Joe stood back, half crouched, his left hand spread stiffly against the air, his mouth pressed up. "Damn you!" he yelled, as he saw the gun, and fired again.

Red Hawk could see the impact of that shot, the shudder that it sent through Jeremy's body; but there seemed to be no killing him. His own bullet he sent home with a much better aim, for he planted it fairly between Joe's eyes so that the dead man fell across the dying.

"The dirty damned skunk! The dirty skunk!" gasped Jeremy.

He writhed his legs together, stretched them out, and lay still.

CHAPTER 30

RED HAWK got to the dead men. He could not reach his own knife with his hands, but he was able to pull out that of Joe. With it he sawed clumsily until he managed to sever the ropes and free himself. Then he sat in the darkening sunset and smoked a pipe to Sweet Medicine. What he felt was not gratitude, but a pure and calm devotion.

Under the stars, under the moon, Red Hawk cut the sod and deepened the grave until it would hold them both, for they must not be allowed to pollute the floor of the house of Sweet Medicine. Then he took their weapons, their wallets, all that was in their pockets, and put the stuff in a saddle bag. When he had finished that, he lay down and slept until the sun was up.

The valley was in perfect peace when he rose. There was no sign of what had happened except the flat, fresh earth of the grave and the torn-up turf where the bank of the creek had been trenched by the shovels of the brothers. These were small wounds, and the rains would touch all into shape again and heal the wounds.

He took the saddle horses and the string of mules on the lead of a rawhide lariat. They pulled out in an awkward line behind him as he rode down the valley until he was in full face of the shining waterfall. There he dismounted and fell on his face in the grass before the bright face and the deep voice of his god. Afterwards he continued slowly down the valley.

It was slow work to bring that train of mules across the hills; it was, in fact, well into the afternoon before he came to the Cheyenne outposts again. What a thing it was to sit his horse on the great hill that overlooked the camp and look down upon the tepees with the knowledge that he was no longer an outcast, but a hero and a maker of mighty medicine to all his tribe. It made him smile, and at the same time there were tears in his eyes.

The scouts saw him as he rode down into the hollow circle of the plain. They did not need to be close in order to see that it was the master of the White Horse who approached the camp. And how they came! Screeching like fiends, and holding their lances above their heads so that the feather streamers stood out stiffly.

He listened to the uproar without smiling, though his heart was smiling, to be sure. Then he saw White Wolf among the rest. He was the brave who had charge of the outposts on this day; a warrior of note, young as he was. His eyes gleamed with pleasure when this great man, this friend of Sweet Medicine, lifted a hand and summoned him. And as he rode beside the white Cheyenne, White Wolf said:

"Did you strike the white men? I see horses for two.

Were there two? I see no scalps, and that is why I ask you!"

Red Hawk paused for a moment. He had not so much as thought of the thing before. For surely he might have counted coup upon the dead, and taken their scalps.

But now he merely said, "It was not I, but Sweet Medicine who killed them. I did not have to lift my hand. Sweet Medicine struck them down by their own hands, when they were about to kill me. I was tied with ropes. I was helpless when Sweet Medicine struck them.

"Since it is the work of Sweet Medicine," said Red Hawk, "the mules, the horses, and everything on them must be returned safely to the whites. I did not win the prizes. Keep them safely for me, White Wolf. Do not let any of the young men or the boys open the packs and steal from them."

At this the warrior laughed a little.

"Do you think that there are fools in the Cheyenne camp?" he asked. "Would not the young men sooner put their hands into fire than touch what is owned by Red Hawk? But it is time that you came back to the camp, because there is need of the strongest medicine that you can make. Spotted Antelope, your father, cannot eat food. He has a fever. Running Elk has done many things, but still your father's face is hot and his hand is dry. Standing Bull and his squaw stay with Spotted Antelope, but now he is talking while his eyes are open and his brain is asleep. It is well that you have come!"

That was the news which brought Red Hawk sweeping into the camp. Before the Cheyennes had fairly heard the news of his coming, he was at the lodge of his father.

Bending Willow sat on one side of the old man, the Blue Bird was on the other, and Standing Bull burned sweet grass and offered up prayers patiently. All three gave a silent greeting to Red Hawk as he kneeled by the old man;

181

the women withdrew to the farther side of the lodge. Standing Bull murmured:

"Running Elk has been here and has gone again, shaking his head. Quickly, brother! It will take a strong medicine to save him. He raves of you and Wind Walker, or Wind Walker and you! Quickly, Red Hawk, because already his breath seems to be rattling in his throat!"

But Red Hawk shook his head. The time was too patently upon Spotted Antelope. The long fasting had wasted away his face, and the gray dust of death was already upon it. One could sorrow for the death of Spotted Antelope, but it seemed impious to wish life back into that worn skeleton. It was only wonderful that breath could still be in him.

But when Red Hawk spoke, the eyes of Spotted Antelope opened and were without the red mist of fever. For that moment his brain was clear.

From under his robe he put out a scrawny hand of ice and laid it, shuddering, in the grip of his foster-son.

"So!" he said. "So! All will be well!" and he closed his eyes with such a smile that Red Hawk thought the ancient brave had hopes of living. But in fact he was only gathering thought and strength for his next words, which he muttered as he opened his eyes again, saying: "My son, between you and Wind Walker let there be peace!"

"There can be no peace with him," said Red Hawk.

"For twenty years," said Spotted Antelope, "I have seen the thing happen, and my son in the hands of Wind Walker. It must not be!"

"Have no fear," said Red Hawk. "Sweet Medicine is close to me. I cannot come to harm."

"But if you injure him, you will come to harm," gasped Spotted Antelope. "It is better for you to die than to kill him."

"Kill him?" said Red Hawk, bewildered. "What dream have you had, father? But there is fever in you. Now close your eyes and sleep, while I sit here beside you and pray to Sweet Medicine—"

"When I close my eyes, I shall be dead!" said Spotted Antelope.

In his excitement, he thrust himself up on one elbow and grasped at Red Hawk's deerskin jacket with his other hand. He seemed in the very act of expiring as he gasped out:

"If you kill him, your ghost will never find rest after death. Better for a brave to lose his shield and his medicine bag and his scalp than for you to kill him. Do you hear me? He is—"

The strength went out of him suddenly. Red Hawk was barely in time to catch the body that spilled inert into his arms. But there was a last tremor of the lips, and the breath of a dying man is sacred. Red Hawk put his ear close to hear the final word, but all that he could make out was a thin murmur that sounded in his ear like "Father— father—" several times repeated.

There was no struggle. Spotted Antelope simply caught his breath, and then breathed no more.

East of the camp there was a hill on which stood a tree. The hill was like a buffalo lying down, and in the tree that stood on top of it, Red Hawk had the burial platform built.

He saw to everything. Bending Willow and the Blue Bird did the work of wrapping the body, but he had laid out the articles which were to go with the corpse—things of such value that sometimes the dark eyes of the two women stole toward him with a question before they enclosed another treasure in the great bundle. For there were two pipes of the red pipestone, one of them so curiously carved that it was considered a tribal treasure. There was a fine bundle of

183

arrows in a cougar-skin case, a new rifle, ammunition, a pair of fine axes, no less than half a dozen knives, a hatchet, the medicine bag, and Spotted Antelope's shield and lance. A flute, a rattle, a buffalo mask, a necklace of the claws of a grizzly bear were added. Then, in five buffalo robes with a valuable painted robe next to the body, the corpse was wrapped. The body was taken outside and lashed on a travois which was pulled away by the best horse in the old man's herd, a fine little steel-dust stallion.

The platform in the tree had already been built. It was hard to lift the clumsy bundle up to it, but finally the thing was done. Then Red Hawk saw that the saddle and the bridle on the stallion were the best that could be found, and finally he ended the ceremony by shooting the horse through the head. It fell not on its side but in a heap, as though struggling to get up. That was very good luck, and it meant that the ghost of the dead man would be well served forever by the ghost of the horse.

Afterwards Red Hawk sat on the brow of the hill for two days and thought of the dead old man. Then he returned to the village.

Red Hawk went to the tepee of Lazy Wolf, but to his amazement that lodge had disappeared. When he inquired, he was told that the tepee had already been packed and was far off on the plain, winding along the trail.

He got on the White Horse and went in pursuit like streaking light.

As Red Hawk drew near, he saw the white man climb down from the wagon and come back down the trail. There he encountered Red Hawk, who threw himself down from the white stallion and grasped the hand of his old friend.

"What does it mean, Lazy Wolf?" he asked. "You go

away without saying good-bye."

"I left you a letter in the hands of Standing Bull," said Lazy Wolf. "It was better to go off without seeing you. It was a lot better."

"Why was it better?" asked Red Hawk.

"Women," said Lazy Wolf, "drove me away from my own people; and it's a woman who drives me back to them again. I don't know everything that's in her mind, but I know that it is time to go."

"She is driving on," said Red Hawk. "And yet she knows you are on foot. That is strange!"

"She's driving on, and that's why I can't stay here to spend a long time yarning with you, Red Hawk," said the other. "I'll have to hurry two miles, now, to catch up with her."

"But what is the matter with her?" asked Red Hawk.

"There is a great pain in her heart," said Lazy Wolf calmly.

"That is very bad. Can Running Elk do anything for her?"

"Only one man in the world can do anything for her. And she doesn't want to see him. Good-bye, Red Hawk. I'm trying to wish you more luck than you are likely to have when you run into Wind Walker. Pray to Sweet Medicine and shoot straight!"

"But wait!" cried Red Hawk, as his friend turned. "Let me ride ahead and stop Blue Bird, so that she'll wait for you. I must say good-bye to her!"

"She has said good-bye to you already," answered the father. "And she won't want to see you now. Don't follow us, my lad."

"But what am I to understand?" cried Red Hawk.

"A few years from now you'll open your eyes—if you're

still wearing a scalp and walking the ground. Then you'll understand all about it," said Lazy Wolf, and he began to jog along after the disappearing wagon.

CHAPTER 31

AMONG the Cheyennes a man was judged by acts, not words. That was why the tribe felt that the grief of Red Hawk for the death of his foster-father was greater than anything that had ever been known before, because he gave away the possessions in the lodge of Spotted Antelope, down to the skins of the lodge itself. There was at least a small pouring of powder or a small handful of the best of bright beads for every man, woman, or child in the camp.

At night, he sat by and watched Dull Hatchet and Standing Bull in war paint lead the dance with every eye in the camp looking on. A war party against the Pawnees would start soon. As for Red Hawk, it was sufficient if he smoked and watched. For he had at last achieved his place in the tribe. For the first time in these many years, Red Hawk was content, for he had found his people and his people had found him.

White Wolf took the possessions of the two dead Bailey brothers into the town of Witherell. He was equipped with a letter to Richard Lester in which Red Hawk had written, briefly, that the two white men had quarreled with one another and that they were both dead. All their goods were being sent back so that the white men could see that the hands of Red Hawk were clean.

The important thing for Red Hawk to decide, at this

time, was whether or not he would accompany the war party that was to strike the Pawnees. There was a rumor that Wind Walker was even now among the Pawnees; and the great goal of Red Hawk's actions must be, now, to come to grips with the famous white man.

But he was by no means sure that Wind Walker was in fact among the Pawnees. Therefore he waited from day to day until he might receive a sign from Sweet Medicine.

So he came to the last evening before Dull Hatchet and the rest were to start on the trail—forty braves chosen from the best.

The camp had fallen asleep peacefully. But a moment after Red Hawk had closed his eyes, there was a murmur and then a sudden outbreak of howling and barking from the dogs. Through this cut the sound of rifles. Red Hawk came out of his tepee with a loaded gun in his hands.

The moon was westering. It shone through a thin haze. Rifles glinted here and there, but what Red Hawk noticed first of all was that the White Horse was not in front of the lodge! He was gone—like a part of Red Hawk's body —and yonder, in the press of the stampeding horses, there was the gleam of the great white crest which tossed like the foam of a wave above the rest of the tumult.

A man sat on the back of the monster. That was what staggered Red Hawk so that he stood helplessly staring. It could not be that the White Horse had submitted to the rule of any other hand than his own!

A great cry was rising from the Cheyennes.

"Wind Walker! Wind Walker!" they were shouting.

That name made Red Hawk groan. What other men were unable to do, Wind Walker could easily accomplish, even to the mastering of the White Horse.

Red Hawk borrowed the first pony at hand, without asking for the owner. He clipped a saddle over the back of the little horse, and, rifle in hand, was carried out of the camp on the heels of a cloud of avengers which had blown from among the tepees.

He could not get full speed out of his mount. He was accustomed to the White Horse, as to a great river of wind that carried a man easily over plains or mountains. Yet something more than the horse was carrying him along. He hardly knew why there was such a feeling of Fate upon him. He only knew that he never would turn back from this trail until he had the White Horse between his knees again.

He heard the rapid thunder of the hoofs, speeding away with half the wealth of the Cheyenne camp. From voices that yelled in rage and hate now and again, he knew that the raid had been made by Pawnees, headed by Wind Walker.

Red Hawk began to laugh, for it seemed plain to him now that Fate was working again, and that the hand of Sweet Medicine was driving him on. Had not all of this been devised in order to include him, with or without his will, in the raid against Wind Walker?

CHAPTER 32

Every day brought a forced march from dawn to dark. The dust kept twisting up in thin, acrid spirals. The sun pressed down harder and harder with the weight of its heat, wasting the flesh from the horses and thumbing out hollows in the faces of the riders. But they went on silently, enduring.

They traveled rapidly, but sometimes they seemed to Red Hawk like so many ants painfully crawling beneath the vast blue arch of the sky.

Hard as the Cheyennes rode, Wind Walker and his Pawnees still receded safely before them, out of the plains and into the hills. And at last the pursuers had full sight of the Pawnees in a position which was so entirely safe that the Cheyennes could merely gather on a hilltop and stare down at the picture with greedy eyes.

The camp was in the center of a huge bowl, with highlands scattered around it. A twist of water ran through the center of the bowl, golden in the evening light. A few trees and shrubs offered fuel, but there was not enough for shelter behind which the camp could be stalked. An attack would have to sweep over a mile of open country to get at those Pawnees. And though there were fewer of them than of the Cheyennes, such an attack would lead to a senseless butchery, with no hope of success.

In the midst of the Pawnee camp there was one figure of shining white that Red Hawk could not take his eyes from —the White Horse.

He said nothing to his companions, but rode straight down the slope. Standing Bull called out a word of warning; but the rest were still as Red Hawk advanced on his thin-shouldered mustang towards the Pawnee camp. He had left his rifle behind him, and he carried no other weapon except the knife with its sixteen-inch blade of fine steel.

As he drew closer to the enemy, he lifted his right hand, palm out, and so advanced the horse at a walk. The Pawnees stood up and stared at him. He was quite close when a voice yelled:

"The Red Hawk!"

A young brave snatched up a rifle and levelled it. Wind

Walker spoke, and the rifle gradually lowered from his aim. That was how Red Hawk rode into the camp of the Pawnees. They were chosen warriors, every one of those roach-headed wolves of the plains, but great and grim as they were, young and old shrank back from the path of this famous Cheyenne medicine man with the white skin.

The White Horse neighed suddenly, and came charging through the group. The stallion followed Red Hawk, nuzzling at his shoulder. The horses neighed again and again, like a great deafening horn.

But Red Hawk could not take notice of the shining monster. He had to step forward as though he were unattended, not letting his eyes dwell on the bloody marks of the bit on the mouth of the great horse, no matter how his heart swelled. With straightforward eyes Red Hawk approached Wind Walker.

The white man stood with his hands on his hips, his hat off, his long hair pouring down over his neck in a dusty sweep. He said quietly:

"Well, Cheyenne? A good many of these Pawnee hands are aching to get at your throat. Is it wise for you to be here? Sit down and eat something—and smoke, and tell me why you've come."

Red Hawk ate with them, and wondered why the food did not choke him. He smoked of the pipe which was passed around the circle afterwards.

Red Hawk took care not to look back over his shoulder at the gleaming image of the White Horse as he said:

"There can be no peace between Wind Walker and the Cheyennes, but even the snake and the owl may live in one house and fair exchanges make both the traders rich. You have a horse, Wind Walker, and I have gold, which is the white man's god. Give me the horse and I will give you as much gold as you can lift from the ground. In the

190

course of one moon, I shall bring the gold to an appointed place and take the horse. Do you listen?"

"As much gold as a man can lift?" said Wind Walker. He gathered his brows and considered Red Hawk. "How many traders have you murdered, then, Red Hawk?"

"The great spirit, Sweet Medicine, struck the ground before me, and the gold lay at my feet," said Red Hawk.

He heard a little intake of breath as the Pawnees listened, but the white man was smiling.

"Well," said Wind Walker, "if there were a thousand mule-loads of gold on one side, and the White Horse on the other, I would keep the horse. You know that there are a lot of good things in the world, my lad, but nothing that pleases me as much as Cheyenne scalps. And the White Horse will help to shorten my time between scalps."

The Pawnees looked silently at the ground. A guest ought not to be insulted and threatened.

Wind Walker's speech was so very bad that Red Hawk stood up. Behind him the White Horse snuffed at his hair and sent a tingle down his spine, but he could not notice the stallion even now.

"In the Cheyenne lodges," said Red Hawk, making his last appeal, "there are better things than gold. They are painted robes and new rifles and plenty of powder and lead. Name what you wish, and I shall bring you guns and robes and many bright new knives. I shall bring you, also, a whole horse-load of sugar and tea. That is a good price for the White Horse."

The Wind Walker merely smiled again and pointed. "You have a bellyful of meat and a brainful of smoke. Go back to the other Cheyenne dogs. The day will come soon when I shall tie your red scalp to the bit of the White Horse—and make him like the smell of it!"

Incredulity came over Red Hawk as he heard the brutality of this speech. But he said, merely:

"Even in the tall sky there is not room enough for two eagles to pass, if they have strong hearts. We shall meet again."

Then he turned and went back to his mustang. The White Horse tried to follow. But many ropes snared him. He began to kick and plunge. As Red Hawk rode off he shuddered, forcing himself to keep from turning. But it seemed as though the rawhide ropes that restrained the stallion were searing his own flesh!

CHAPTER 33

THREE days later the Pawnees vanished from the hills like a thin cloud from beneath the hot face of the sun. Dull Hatchet could find only the general direction of the flight. The reason of it was clear enough. No doubt Wind Walker had kept the band together all this time in the hope that the Cheyennes might walk into some ambuscade. Failing in that chance, the Pawnees had been sent off—the greater part of them at least—to take the encumbering herd of stolen horses back to the Pawnee camps. They might return, then, and try to bait Dull Hatchet's band with a greater force.

The Cheyenne chief, learning how the many trails scattered to this side and that, picked out a northern landmark, a tall, bar-headed mountain. Then he scattered his entire troop, with directions to regather on the southern slope of the mountain. On the way, one of the men might pick up the trail of the scattered Pawnees.

That was how Red Hawk came to be riding alone on his

scrawny down-headed mustang, through the narrows of a great defile. The sun was directly overhead, scalding him, when he heard a dull, bumping sound, and the horse dropped flat on the earth beneath him. An instant later the report of the rifle came welling down into the cañon as Red Hawk rolled away from the body of the dead mustang and into the shade of a boulder.

Over the edge of that boulder he looked up and saw the silhouette of the White Horse, racing on the verge of the cliff against the sky, with Wind Walker sitting huge in the saddle. The White man-slayer thought, no doubt, that the fall of the horse was what had flung Red Hawk out of the saddle and behind the barrier of the rock. Perhaps he was looking now for a way to ride down the rough sandstone steps of the side of the valley, and so get at his victim.

Then Red Hawk's whistle, that had called the White Horse many times, went up thin as the scream of a hawk. He saw the sound strike the stallion. He saw the shining form whirl and leap from the top ledge to a lower level, and again to another narrow platform of rock. Down came the White Horse, with Wind Walker struggling vainly to arrest that descent. It was all the rider could do to keep his place.

Red Hawk, his heart filled with laughter, snatched up his fallen rifle and levelled it. He would not shoot until that target was so close that there was no danger of striking the horse instead of the man. Then, on the very lowest shelf of the descent, he saw Wind Walker slung sidelong from the horse. Down he came, his body spinning rapidly over and over, until he lay motionless on the red shale that covered the bottom of the ravine. And here was the White Horse, at last, with a thin cloud of dust sweeping behind him as he galloped to his master, a red froth flying back from his torn mouth and onto his chest and shoulders.

Red Hawk spoke one joyous word to the horse as he ran forward. Then he saw Wind Walker rise up from the ground. From a ragged tear in his scalp, blood ran down over one side of the white man's face. He staggered on uncertain feet.

Something in that gesture—the hopelessness of even those mighty hands warding away the flying bullet—made the heart of Red Hawk change. He remembered, suddenly, how once he had awakened from a deathlike trance and found himself outside Wind Walker's house. His life had been spared, then.

And so he stood back, his rifle ready, but grasped only in his right hand while with his left he stroked the quivering neck of the White Horse.

The Wind Walker came suddenly to his full senses. He dragged the back of his hand across his face, and through the blood that was clotting on his forehead, he peered forth at his enemy.

"I was once in your hands," said Red Hawk. "Instead of killing me, you threw me out of your house. You let the life grow up in me once more. The Cheyennes have asked the spirits to let them have your scalp, but Sweet Medicine has given me back the White Horse, and that is enough to take, even from a great spirit, in one day. Farewell!"

He mounted the White Horse. He could not believe that he was riding deliberately away from the glory of killing that great foe of the Cheyennes.

When he looked back he saw Wind Walker in the same place, no longer staggering, but with fallen head, like one whose spirit had been overwhelmed. Yet they would meet again, and the next meeting would certainly be the end of their feud.

He felt no pride in that encounter. Chance and the

White Horse had brought Wind Walker to his feet, and with a truly Cheyenne terseness he merely said to the others, that night at the camp:

"Wind Walker is still alive!"

His red brothers eyed the stallion with wonder, and said nothing.

They had entered now into a deadly game of tiger-hunt-tiger. Through a labyrinth of cañons, broken mesas, sharp-sided hills, the hunt continued.

But the patience of the Indians was soon exhausted, and one after another the Cheyennes melted away to return to the distant camp. At last there remained only a grim trio; men hard as metal and welded together like steel—Dull Hatchet, Standing Bull, and Red Hawk.

The Pawnees, they knew, had scattered also. There was only a small group of them remaining, but among those Wind Walker was sure to be found.

They were in the jumble of a gigantic "bad lands." Water flowed in most of these gorges only after heavy rains, when the erosion went on rapidly. During the rest of the year only the wind was at work, with its chisels of flying sand hewing the rocks and wearing away more rapidly the clay slopes.

Standing Bull said, "Here all the red tribes could be hidden so that even a hawk would have a hard time to find a single man. But we must search. Red Hawk, may your medicine be strong!"

Wind Walker hovered like a hawk in all their minds, night and day.

Dull Hatchet established a system that showed why he was war chief of the tribe. His method was slow, but it was sure. It consisted of placing one man on the highest eminence in sight so that he could act as lookout while the others scouted through the ravines below, ever and anon looking up towards their spy, who was ready to warn them by signals if he chanced to spot the enemy in the distance.

It was slow, painful, and anxious work, and they spent days at it. The weather was hot and windless. For food they crunched parched corn and chewed jerked venison, washed down with tainted water from the stagnant water-holes. Every day their bodies burned dry and their eyes sank back beneath their brows, wrinkled pouches of skin gathering around the lids.

Since the bright sheen of the White Horse began to seem like a shining light that would be sure to take the eye of the enemy from afar, his coat was smudged over with yellow and brown clay.

Altogether, they were in the bad lands seven days. And in the late afternoon of the seventh, Red Hawk made his way stealthily down the bottom of a dry ravine. For some time he had not looked back toward the lookout which Dull Hatchet was keeping from the top of a flat hill behind him. Coming to a stretch of still water that had not the least film of green over it, he tasted it. It was strongly alkaline, therefore he drank only sparingly of it. Nevertheless, it was time that the empty water skins were refilled, so he turned back to signal the discovery to the lookout.

Then it was that he saw on the top of the mesa, through the burning, golden haze of the slanting afternoon light, the brief and shadowy flickering of an arm. It said, almost as swiftly as speech: "Come in! Enemy! Come in!"

CHAPTER 34

THE many days of hunting collapsed to a moment, only, on the instant that Red Hawk's eye deciphered that signal. He turned and ran back, his body bent horizontal and in his ears the imagined clang of a distant rifle, the thin whine of a bullet.

When he came to the foot of the mesa, Standing Bull and Dull Hatchet were already there, Dull Hatchet on one knee, loading his rifle. He had thrown off his deerskin shirt and flung away his leggings, so that he was in a breechclout only. To Red Hawk he looked the mightiest figure of a man he had ever seen. What was even Wind Walker compared with this copper-skinned giant?

Standing Bull, stripped to the waist, was hardly less imposing. What he lacked in height and weight, he made up in an appearance of greater agility.

Dull Hatchet stood up and pointed.

"Over there toward the hill with the two tops," he said, "there is a mesa with a flat top. On it I saw the shine of the sun on a medicine glass. It is a hunter, and the game he hunts is not deer or antelope or buffalo. He is hunting men!"

Red Hawk had quite forgotten the possibility that Wind Walker might have with him a field glass.

"We must go ahead quickly and carefully," Dull Hatchet continued. "The white man may have seen me wave from the top of the rock. He may be waiting with others, and they may be loading their rifles with new bullets and smiling at one another. Ahead of us, a little distance, there is another high hill that looks out on two cañons. Let us climb it. Tether the ponies to the White Horse, because he knows how to stand still."

"Suppose Wind Walker goes by us, following another ravine, and so comes out behind us and catches the horses," said Standing Bull.

"At a time like this," answered Dull Hatchet, "one stupid mind is better than three clever ones. I have thought of one way to try to fight them; but we have no time to talk about it. While we sit in a council, the white men are perhaps stealing towards us."

They did as he said, because the point of his last remark was perfectly patent. Standing Bull tethered the other ponies to the White Horse, while Red Hawk stood in front of the stallion and talked to him quietly.

Now the swift feet of the Cheyennes found the way down the cañon until they came to the foot of that hill which the chief had discovered before. All its lower slopes were deeply gullied red clay; above, there was a flat cap of rock, turreted like a castle, so that the place made a perfect citadel.

They climbed until they had reached an upper brow of the rock. There were other hilltops not far away from which they could be seen, and so they crawled to the forward edge of the big stone platform. Lying flat, over the edge of the rock Red Hawk could see right down into the right-hand ravine where, coming towards them, were three men. He had a glimpse of one, then another, and another.

"Back! Back!" said Dull Hatchet.

They wormed back from the edge of the platform. Dull Hatchet was saying in a murmur, "Keep well in. From time to time I shall look over the edge of the rock. Did you see?"

"I saw the roached heads of the Pawnee wolves," said Standing Bull.

"Good!" said Red Hawk.

But to him Wind Walker was the great prize. When he thought of the fixed and savage light in the eye of the famous man-slayer, his breath left his body.

Dull Hatchet went on, "There is a place where the ravine has no rough places—no brush, no rocks, and no hollows. If they cross that close together they will all be in sight at once, and we shall try to shoot. Keep close here to the edge of the rock. Have your rifles ready. When I give the word, be ready to push the guns over and fire. I shall take Wind Walker. You, Standing Bull, take whichever of the Pawnees is on the right. Red Hawk, take the man on his left."

Red Hawk had to remember that unless they took this advantage, now that they had won it, the enemy would be perfectly ready to slaughter them. The whole fame of Wind Walker rested on the fact that he fought Indians by the use of Indian methods. Only the interposition of Sweet Medicine had induced him to spare Red Hawk's life on that other day.

Another thing, however, suddenly began to beat in Red Hawk's temples. That was the memory of how Spotted Antelope had died, upon his lips a warning to his foster son never to harm Wind Walker. Some dread secret had been in the Cheyenne's throat, but death had choked it.

"Quick!" whispered the war chief.

Red Hawk raised himself on both elbows and settled the butt of his rifle against his right shoulder. Leaning his head to the right, he closed his left eye. Thus he looked down the sights over the rim of the rock, and saw beneath him the three men.

They had come to that bit of unsheltered ground. Off to their left was a deep draw, along its edge a scattering of brush. This would have given them cover, but their caution would have been more than human had they wormed their way through that jagged cut instead of taking the upper ground.

Even so, it was plain that the two Pawnees did not like this business of crossing open ground. Wind Walker's lofty, stately form strode along as though he had no fear of bullets, but the two Indians skulked forward, constantly edging toward the right, to get to cover again more quickly. They were both to the right of Wind Walker, for which reason Dull Hatchet corrected his directions rapidly, saying:

"Take the one nearest the side of the ravine, Red Hawk."

Red Hawk had the figure in his sights, an easy, point-blank shot. He could not miss, though for that rifle he had to allow of a bit of driftage to the left. He made that correction; but he felt that he wanted more time. He felt, somehow, that he had been hurried into this.

Then the man he covered looked suddenly up, froze in place, and the sun flashed on his arm as he pointed.

Red Hawk squeezed the trigger at the same instant. The rifles on either side of him roared in a double report even before his own weapon spoke. His Pawnee bounded into the air, turning round and round like a dancer. He landed in a heap, his arms sprawling out to either side, and lay still. Off to his left, the other Pawnee had fallen.

But Wind Walker had bounded to one side as the bullet struck him—or so it seemed—and had been caught in the brush at the verge of the draw. His broad hat could be seen there, at least.

Standing Bull's yell sounded far away in the ears of Red Hawk. "Sweet Medicine steadied our rifles!" he was shouting joyfully.

"I go to climb the higher rock behind us," Dull Hatchet said. "From that place I can look farther and see if any other men are coming!"

He went back swiftly, calling over his shoulder the suggestion that the other two put at least one more bullet into each of the fallen men. Standing Bull hardly needed that cautioning. He had already loaded, well before Red Hawk.

"This for Wind Walker!" he said as he fired, and Red Hawk distinctly saw the hat in the brush move.

"Take your own man again!" exclaimed Standing Bull.

"He is dead," said Red Hawk.

Then he saw the second Pawnee, the one that Standing Bull had struck down in the first place, push himself up into a sitting posture and try to crawl away. But it seemed as though his legs were glued to the ground.

"I have him!" shouted Standing Bull, reloading again with flying hands.

"Let him be!" said Red Hawk. "Look! He is dying again. He is singing the death-song, brother!"

For up from the ravine came the small, wavering sound of the chant. By the pauses in it, it seemed to Red Hawk that he could count the pulses of agony, the dragging steps by which life departed from the wounded man.

"Let him die before his song is finished," said Standing Bull, and levelled his rifle once more.

Red Hawk grasped his arm.

"Let him die in peace," he urged. "If the Listeners Above wish to hear him, let him finish his song."

Standing Bull turned a convulsed face. "Are you a woman, still?" he exclaimed.

But turning suddenly aside, he took a fresh aim and fired again at the broad hat which was stuck in the brush at the side of the draw beneath them.

To Red Hawk's amazement, that hat turned to the side, revealing the fact that there was no head beneath it; and then it dropped quite out of view.

Standing Bull grunted with alarm. "Suppose he was not killed, brother!" said he. "Suppose he leaped into the draw when the rifles sounded, and that Dull Hatchet missed him! Suppose nothing happened to him, except that his hat was stuck there in the brush?"

Red Hawk stared back at his friend. "Then," said he, "Wind Walker might still be alive and running up that draw or down it, unseen by us and ready to fire?"

Standing Bull nodded, and the two looked gloomily at one another.

"We must go back and tell Dull Hatchet," said Standing Bull; and rising, they hurried back to the rear of that shoulder of rock.

Above them rose the turrets another fifty feet or more.

"Do you hear? Dull Hatchet!" called Standing Bull.

"I hear! I hear!" said Dull Hatchet. "There are no others in sight. We may climb down to the valley now."

"Wind Walker's hat has been knocked out of the brush by two bullets," said Standing Bull. "Perhaps he was not hurt at all, but only left his hat behind. Or perhaps he is lying dead in the bottom of the draw."

There was an exclamation from Dull Hatchet. "There is a bullet through his heart," he vowed, "unless the spirits turned it aside from his flesh. Come, come! We must go down . . ."

His voice changed and rang out suddenly on a note of astonishment and fear. He had been looking down at them through an embrasure in the upper rocks. Now, as he whirled about, Red Hawk had the briefest glimpse of another figure with long gray hair blown over the shoulders, rushing in upon the Cheyenne chief.

202

In an instant they were out of sight.

"Wind Walker!" groaned Standing Bull, and began to bound up the rock like a mountain goat.

CHAPTER 35

It seemed to Red Hawk that two mighty spirits of the upper air were storming against each other high above his head, as he climbed. When he thought of the colossal bulk of Dull Hatchet and his fearless heart, he could not prefigure defeat for the Cheyenne. Yet when he thought of the charging form of Wind Walker, he could no more dream that that man was liable to fail.

With his loaded rifle under his arm, the climbing was slower for him than for Standing Bull, who had thrown down his empty gun and rushed like a hero straight for the battle, with only a knife for weapon. Still he was not far behind. And he had no fear.

That was why the foot of Red Hawk was lightened as he climbed the rock. He was close to the top, with the naked, muscular legs of Standing Bull flashing above him, when he saw the huge bulk of Dull Hatchet forced back to the verge of the upper platform. There he and the Wind Walker whirled for an instant, before the Cheyenne lurched suddenly outward, with a frightful yell. The shadow of his falling body rushed over Red Hawk. As he drew himself up onto the level of the rocks above, he heard the heavy fall below him, and the crunching sound of the breaking bones.

He had even time to wonder at the ability of Wind

Walker—a walker of the wind, indeed, since he had been able to travel out of the draw and climb so quickly to take his enemies in the rear.

Then, as he got to his feet with his rifle, Red Hawk saw Standing Bull leap in with his knife at the enemy, regardless of the jagged fragment of stone which Wind Walker swayed in his hand. The stone moved as if for a blow; Standing Bull swerved to the side and ran in; and then the ruin descended fairly on his head. He went down without a cry, his great body flashing in the sun as he stretched out and lay still.

With some extra sense, though hardly with his eyes, Red Hawk saw this; for his real vision he was using to look down the sights of his rifle at the body of Wind Walker. The giant hesitated for an instant as though he knew that death was inescapable. Then, with a shout, though his hands were empty, he rushed straight forward to receive the bullet.

A red glory of admiration and wonder flowered in the brain of the younger man as he saw the veteran come in at him. He remembered, too, how he had once fallen before the gun of this hero—and had been spared. He could feel, in memory, the red-hot finger of the bullet that ripped the flesh along his head.

He cast his rifle aside, and it fell with a loud clangor on the rocks. For if Sweet Medicine was in fact his protector, what did Red Hawk need of rifles? His own hands would be enough. He gave a wild yell and sprang to meet the charge, even forgetting the great knife in his belt as he reached for the enemy.

His hands grasped at a bulk which seemed to have ribs of rock. And as he dodged to the side, Wind Walker's grasp ripped the deerskin shirt from his back and flung him headlong, half stunned.

All that he knew was that a hand had grasped his long hair, and that he had been half raised so that his neck was bent back over the knee of the giant. One effort of that tremendous arm would shatter his spine. Against the flaring sunlight of the sky he saw the terrible face of Marshall Sabin, and out of the distance he heard the failing voice of the Pawnee raised in the death chant.

"Here!" said Wind Walker. "Here, you damned white-skinned red-hearted murderer of a Cheyenne! Tell me where you got this, and perhaps you'll have two minutes more to live, then you can sing your own death song. Do you hear? Where did you get it?" As he spoke he lifted the green amulet.

Red Hawk's voice was strangled in his throat. Yet even now, in the whirling of his mind, he had time to wonder how even Sweet Medicine could save him now. But he said: "It has always been around my neck, ever since I was a small boy."

Red Hawk found himself lifted to his feet. One of Wind Walker's vast hands still grasped him by the hair; the other pointed over the edge of the rock.

"Dull Hatchet!" exclaimed the Wind Walker thickly. "That murdering devil of a Cheyenne butcher—he is with you today. Is it *his* section of the tribe that you've lived with ever since you can remember?"

"Yes," said Red Hawk.

Wind Walker's hands gripped him suddenly by the elbows, freezing every nerve in his arms to numbness.

"I'm going mad!" gasped Marshall Sabin. "God keep my brain clear! Lad, are you half Indian and half white? Was either your father or mother a Cheyenne?"

"No," said Red Hawk. He looked into the working face of the Wind Walker, and suddenly shuddered from head to foot.

"How long have you been with them? How long have you been with the tribe? Do you know that?"

"Seventeen—eighteen years," said Red Hawk.

Wind Walker's terrible hands released him suddenly. Red Hawk could have snatched out the long knife at his belt and buried it in the body of the white man at that moment, but he heard the giant cry:

"Remember exactly—for God's sake! Was it eighteen years ago?—Was it?"

"It was—exactly eighteen years," nodded Red Hawk. "I have heard them name the year when I was brought to the tribe. Spotted Antelope—"

The pointing, rigid arm of Wind Walker stopped him, the wild eyes that searched his face.

"You once sacrificed a horse on the grave of my dead wife, boy," said Marshall Sabin. "Why did you do that?"

"Because I heard a voice come out of her grave, one day a long time ago."

"What voice? In the name of God, are you going to give me your damned Indian nonsense and spirit chatter now? What did the voice out of the grave say to you?"

"Only one word. It was is if I had remembered it out of some dim past. 'Rusty,' it said. I do not know why."

When a bullet drives straight through the heart, the flesh of the body quivers once and is quiet, and the breath may swell the throat and part the lips once without a sound coming. It seemed to Red Hawk that his last word had so struck through the body of Marshall Sabin and left him, in a moment, still and calm. His man-slaying hand stretched towards Red Hawk with the palm turned up.

"Rusty," said such a voice as Red Hawk never had heard before, "can you see with my eyes? It was your mother's name for you, and you are my son!"

CHAPTER 36

THE death song of the Pawnee in the lower ravine had ended by now. Speech was rising with happiness and sorrow out of Rusty Sabin's throat, and still he listened to the voice of his father.

Standing Bull, however, stirred suddenly and rose. The fallen rifle was instantly in Marshall Sabin's hands, but Rusty said to him:

"This is my friend!" and instantly the mouth of the rifle pointed to the ground.

Somehow they got Standing Bull down the cliff to the ravine and to the horses, where with water from the water bags they washed his wound and bound up his head. He had heard the story, by that time, and when he had recovered from his astonishment enough to take his hand from his mouth, he said:

"Red Hawk, it is the work of Sweet Medicine! Our rifles were charmed. Our knives had not edges to strike into the flesh of Wind Walker. Therefore he was turned into your father so that he may do us no more harm. What will you do?"

"I cannot take my father among the Cheyennes. Therefore I must go with him among the whites," said Red Hawk. "Dull Hatchet lies dead, but he died on the war path, as a good man should. You can count two coups, and you can tell the tribe that you have fought hand to hand with Wind Walker. It is not a bad journey for you."

"*Ah-hai!*" said Standing Bull. "The tribe has lost the war chief, and I have lost my friend. Do you tell me nevertheless to be happy? Go back with me to our people, Red Hawk," he pleaded. "Tell them the truth. Otherwise, if I stand up among them and speak, they will never forget that I went out on the war path with Dull Hatchet and with the friend of Sweet Medicine. They will never forgive me. Bad luck will be seen where my shadow falls. Come back with me, and say farewell to the tribe, if you must go!"

Even Wind Walker could understand the necessity for that journey, and so they headed slowly out of the hills and across the plains, letting the horses gather strength, and dressing the wound of Standing Bull every day so that only the scar remained when he reached the camp.

Outside the camp, Marshall Sabin took the hand of his son and said:

"Is it safe for you to go in? The treacherous red devils may forget what you've been to them, the moment they learn you're my son. They may cut your throat for you!"

Rusty Sabin looked back into that grim face and answered very gravely, "My skin is white, and you are my father—but all my life the Cheyennes are my people!"

Marshall Sabin's big head wagged in wonder. He never would understand, Rusty could see.

Through the twilight Red Hawk rode out of the hills with Standing Bull, and into the noise of the camp. He went swiftly, secretly, to his lodge, leaving Standing Bull to spread the news. And while Red Hawk stripped himself to the breechclout and painted himself blue and yellow, he heard the evening commotion as it swept in waves through the camp. Far away, he heard the yell of the mourning women begin; those were the squaws of Dull Hatchet, lamenting their dead.

He took special care, finally, in painting all across his breast the likeness of a flying owl, in red.

He walked out to the great fire, stalking along behind his friend. Old Hopping Bird came out of a waiting cluster of people and threw herself down before him. Her grandson Gray Eagle was dying, she said, unless help came to him from the Sky People. They had the boy there in a litter, and by the light of a torch Red Hawk could see the starved and wasted face. They pulled back the buffalo robe and showed the whole body, thin as a corpse that has dried for months under a parching sun. The lad was fourteen, and the frightful scars of the initiation had never healed perfectly.

Gray Eagle's glazed eyes now shone with sudden hope. He smiled and lifted an uncertain hand toward the friend of Sweet Medicine. Red Hawk dropped to his knees; he laid his hands on the great knotted scars of the initiation. Then he felt something go out of him; he could feel virtue flowing down his arms and through his hands. Perhaps this would be his last deed among the Cheyennes. Words came slowly from his lips:

"Sweet Medicine is near me. I feel his breathing. His strength goes through me into the body of Gray Eagle. Peace shall enter Gray Eagle's veins. Strength shall flow into him. He shall live!"

Hopping Bird gave a cry of joy. Red Hawk stood up. And he heard the boy muttering:

"It is true! I shall live. I felt the life come into me when I heard the voice of the medicine man."

Red Hawk said, "What have you done for him, Hopping Bird?"

"All that the wise men advised. He has had a fever. We have given him sweat baths twice a day. We have carried him down and plunged him in the river afterwards, when

209

he was too weak to walk. Still he grows weaker."

Red Hawk thought of the stifling steam of the sweat-house and sighed.

"Sweet Medicine has entered his body," he said. "Give him no more baths. Let him be very quiet. Hush the children near the tepee. Give him buffalo tongues and boiled corn—a little every day. In the morning and the evening, sing a chant to Sweet Medicine. You need not lift your voice very high; you will be heard."

Then he went away, and behind him he heard the people laughing with joy. And he heard the voice of the boy saying again:

"I shall live! I feel the strength in me!"

But the strength had run out of Red Hawk, and he was weak. His knees bent under him as he strode out into the light of the bonfire and saw about him, once again, the thick circle of the listeners.

As he dropped the robe from his shoulders a murmur rose. Hands pointed towards the painting on his breast. He saw a young squaw lift up her son so that the boy could see the prodigy.

"The sign of Sweet Medicine!" she said.

With his head thrown back, Red Hawk looked at the stars, and a great silence fell over the camp, except where the wives of Dull Hatchet lamented, far away. The voice of their grief entered rhythmically into him, and it seemed to be his own soul that was crying out.

At last he said: "There is grief in me like the sorrow that puffs up the body of a small child. I must go away. My father waits for me; his blood calls to me. I go out among the white people. I must eat their food, but the spirit behind my teeth will always be Cheyenne. Every day I shall turn toward you and pray to Sweet Medicine to give you happiness. The white people have given me a new name—

but keep one place in your heart, and let Red Hawk be there. I hope the sadness that fills me now is a sorrow that I shall take away from the tribe. Sickness and famine, and the longing for peace; that is what I carry away. I leave joy behind me. Let me touch all of you with my hands. Oh, my brothers and sisters! . . ."

He could not talk any longer. He walked like a blind man, slowly, with Standing Bull at his side, guiding him through the crowd.

At the edge of the village the crowd halted as though at a wall. Only Standing Bull took three forward paces, and stood beside the sheen of the White Horse and the departing man. He gripped the hands of Red Hawk and repeated the old formula of the blood brothers:

"Your blood is my blood; my blood is your blood. Your life is my life: my life is your life."

Red Hawk spoke the same words. He could only whisper them.

When he had mounted, the White Horse seemed to understand, and went away on soft, careful feet. Behind them the tribe began to sing, with the great voices of men and the sweet voices of the women and children, the lament for the missing:

> "One arrow—one arrow—one arrow . . .
> One arrow has gone forth . . .
> Return, O arrow! Return to me!" . . .

Red Hawk never once turned his head, but when the singing died away in the distance, it seemed to him that the night grew suddenly darker.

211

CHAPTER 37

On that long journey across the plains, bright and bare as the sea, the father and the son rarely spoke to one another. They were constrained and self-conscious; they used towards one another a scrupulous politeness.

Sometimes, when Rusty Sabin looked at his father, he felt a sudden sting of pity in his eyes. For he could feel that the mere fact of blood had made Marshall Sabin love him, and in his own heart he was sure that he never could feel a natural affection for Wind Walker, the slayer of his red brothers.

Yet it was Rusty who stopped, on the way down Witherell Creek, at the obscure ruins of the shack; and it was Rusty who dismounted from the White Horse and stood beside the white grave stone. Then he told his father how he had first found the place.

Marshall Sabin pulled off his hat. He was perfectly calm as Rusty talked about her. All the way across the plains the elder white man had not once mentioned his dead wife, but only now was Rusty conscious of the omission.

He heard how Marshall Sabin, on that day those years ago, had left the small house and the cornfield, and how he had returned in the dusk of the day to find his house half wrecked, his cornfield trampled as though by blind beasts, and on the earth floor the body of his dead wife.

"But there was no pain in her face, Rusty," said Marshall Sabin. "She looked even younger than she had when I married her. And it must have been because of that look on her face that the Cheyennes did not scalp her. She had long red hair, Rusty, the same color as yours. Yet they hadn't scalped her," he repeated.

"And you were gone. Of course I thought you were dead. I kept on thinking that till I saw the green beetle hanging from your neck the other day. She used to wear that beetle on a cord that passed around her hair. It looked pretty there—the green against the red."

It seemed to Rusty Sabin that there was not enough air in the world for him to breathe. When his mind cleared, afterward, it was as though the Cheyennes had withdrawn to a distance. Yes, it was as though the great red tribe had been seen marching off into the horizon, with the White Indian, Red Hawk, among them.

Looking into Marshall Sabin's face, so marked by the long years of pain, he saw the Wind Walker no longer. In his place was the big-shouldered, fearless young man who had leaned over his dead wife in the cabin with terrible resolves growing up in his brain like the smoke of a sacrificial fire.

"I pick up these years one by one," said Rusty at last. "I put them behind me. I begin again at that time when you came home and found the empty house, Father."

They left at once, and rode on towards Witherell. They could talk, now. There was that matter of the gold, about which Marshall Sabin was naturally very curious, but the mention of it brushed a swift shadow across the face of his son.

"I have turned my back on my people. They are lost to me," said Rusty sadly. "Do not ask me to send my thoughts back to them for the sake of gold."

Marshall Sabin said no more. He permitted the conversation to run on the subject of the girl, a theme that grew like a river in flood, with Rusty talking. And it did not fail until they entered the town and came to the house of Richard Lester.

"Go in to them, Father," said Rusty. "I am ashamed to see them because they know that I have offered them money and that I come for the girl, to make her my squaw. Talk to them, and then let me know what they say."

Said the father, "I know a good deal about this thing. Lester has talked to me because he knows of the night you came to my house. He will let the girl be as free as the wind. She may do as she pleases."

"Good!" said Rusty. "But since her father is sick and her mother is weak, he must come with us. And you, also, my father. Because of her parents, we must go to a southern land, where there is more sun and where the wind cannot blow cold. Only go in quickly and speak to them. Tell the girl that the White Horse is here, and that I am waiting with the horse."

Marshall Sabin, for a moment, rested his hand on the shoulder of his son. Then he strode up the path and passed around to the rear of the house. Rusty heard the knock of the hand against the door, the creak of the hinges, the sound of voices, the shutting of the door, and silence again.

Then, listening closely, he could hear inside the house his father's deep, swelling voice. He heard tingling outcries break in upon that voice, but he gave little attention to them.

At last the deep voice paused, and presently the front door of the house opened. He could not see who came down the steps; in his ears there was a mighty rushing, like the thunder of a cataract in the Sacred Valley that the White Indian had heard.

Stepping back, he leaned his right arm up on the neck of the stallion. Then a hand touched him.

"Rusty!" said the voice of Maisry Lester. "Come into the house!"

He closed his eyes.

"No," said he, "because you have come to stay with me—forever."

If she stepped back now, he felt, she was lost to him. So, with his eyes still shut, he put out his left arm, found her, and drew her in close to him. Then he opened his eyes. She had said nothing, because she needed to say nothing. Neither of them moved. But Rusty felt that they were rushing together out of the world of flesh, and that they were sweeping through a measureless domain of the spirit.

He took one of her hands in his and felt its smallness, its warmth and strength. It seemed to fit exactly his grasp, as though he could compass her, body and soul.

They sailed on the next river steamer that left Witherell. The plan was to take Richard Lester as quickly as possible down the Mississippi to New Orleans, and then trek westward into the land of bright skies and little rain about which Rusty had often heard.

It was easily arranged. That gold which Rusty had brought in had, in fact, almost the power of a god; and it enabled them to start at once on the journey. On the day when they sailed, the entire town knocked off work to see the departure, and there were cheers when the White Horse went up the gangway, making a final spring onto the deck that sent out a sound like a great drum beaten.

Rusty was busy quieting the horse. Later on, the stallion could be worked back to the stall that had been prepared for him. In the meantime, steam was gotten up and the ship began to tremble with the life of the raging wood fires that sent the sparks rushing high into the air and sent

215

blazing cinders blowing out toward the dock. The horse stood with the people at the end of the deck, sometimes throwing up his head to look about him with terrified eyes, and again sniffing for reassurance at Rusty's face.

Mrs. Lester, in tears, was waving frantically to her many acquaintances. Richard Lester, a fragile form leaning on the arm of the gigantic Marshall Sabin, made an occasional gesture toward a friend. He was very happy; but even if he had been sad, the bursting joy of Marshall Sabin would have been enough to scatter the darkness from the mind of his friend.

The ropes were cast off. The stern paddle wheel began to groan and turn, dashing into the water. The sky began to move slowly overhead. The voices of the crowds died out. The great engines were carrying Rusty out toward a new life.

He looked toward the girl. She leaned against the rail, at a little distance. Her glance shifted slowly, calmly, from the White Horse to Rusty Sabin. She smiled a little. It was typical of her that she should stand there at a little distance, with the look of one who has plucked a wild bird out of the sky and has made it her own forever.